MICROWAVE IS DEAD

Southern Humor, Strangely Perverse

A Sequel to *Bearing Crosses*

BY PENNY GARDIN LEWIS

Vabella Publishing
P.O. Box 1052
Carrollton, Georgia 30112
www.vabella.com

Cover Illustration Copyright © 2017 by C. Louise Garrett (Gentry)

Chapter Opening and Closing Photographs © 2017 Penny Lewis

Poetry of Claire Baker and Eleanor Hoomes used by permission.

While some family stories are based on the author's memoirs, this is a work of fiction. Names, characters, businesses, places, events and incidents are either the products of the author's imagination or used in a fictitious manner. Any resemblance to actual persons, living or dead, or actual events is purely coincidental or has been told with the person's permission.

In addition, anyone who knows me is fully aware that I am directionally challenged. I took great liberties in this story with geographical locations and directions in Georgia and Alabama. To the fine folks of Graham, Alabama, I apologize for the totally fictitious description of the crash site.

13-digit ISBN 978-1-942766-42-1

Library of Congress Control Number 2017911954

10 9 8 7 6 5 4 3 2 1

DEDICATION

This book is dedicated to all of my wonderful friends, especially those from PenPals and the Blue Heron Art Studio, who inspire and tolerate me.

And, as always, to my husband, Dan, my daily muse.

ODE TO MICROWAVES

Dearly Beloved, you are a perfect example of form
wed to function. You are electromagnetic radiation
in the microwave frequency range, and you hunker
in pride of place on kitchen counter tops.

Dearly Beloved, you are an electromagnetic radiation
appliance which induces polar molecules to rotate
to produce thermal energy pronto for impatient
connoisseurs of the Ole Quick and Easy.

Your polar molecules rotate, rotate, rotate to provide
hungry gourmets fish sticks and chicken fingers.
Your uniform excitation evenly heats
leftovers in a dielectric heating process.

Dearly beloved by all who know and utilize you,
O, Microwave, your carousel revolves clockwise
until pause, stir, recover, restart-- then counterclockwise.
Ding. Ding. "Come and get it. Lean Cuisine's ready."

Eleanor Wolfe Hoomes   7/10/17

PROLOGUE

The water was cold . . . cold on the skin . . . cold in the mouth . . . cold in the lungs. The little girl fought with all of her six-year-old might against the snarled roots at the bottom of the river that held her ankle. Bending her knee and thrusting, she wriggled free at last, leaving her rubber boot behind. It was too late. She had no breath left to swim to the top. One more gasp . . . one more gulp of the murky water. Her last conscious thought was "Daddy." She couldn't see anymore. Only darkness.

The sparkly pink shirt hung from the low tree branch, catching the light like a lone beacon signaling rescue. It hung there for hours until the heavy winds and rain loosened its hold and sent the shirt flying through the air and into the frigid waters below. The garment, caught in the current, floated more than a mile downstream, finally stopping at a large boulder and mangles of debris in the river's center. The little girl's shirt, like hope, lingered there for days.

CHAPTER 1
I AM NOT A DETECTIVE

Let me make something perfectly clear. Despite solving the mystery of a decapitated head in a salad bowl, WE ARE NOT detectives! But, my crazy twin sister, Pam Hill, thinks we are. We are, in fact, two retired, menopausal, middle-aged women, with grown children and lots of hobbies. Pam was loving . . . reveling in . . . the attention that our story had garnered. For weeks, every time I picked up a newspaper, I would read a story about the adventure of twins Penny and Pam. And a lot of it wasn't even true. Facts were distorted giving us far too much credit. Thankfully, a year had gone by, the buzz had died down, and normal life had resumed . . . for the most part.

Last September, my sister and I had left for an innocent trip to take pictures of roadside cross memorials to help our, perfectly healthy, Mom plan her final wishes. We inadvertently got swept up in the beheading murder of our cousin Jacey's husband, Junebug, in Athens, Tennessee. The two of us were only trying to help Jacey's funny little attorney and a handsome detective gather some of the facts. We, or at least I, had no expectation that we would solve the case. But we did. And we nearly got ourselves killed doing so, mainly because of Pam.

I am fourteen minutes older than my twin, and so, I should be the mature adult in this relationship . . . the leader. But she drags me into trouble even when I know better. It wasn't always this way.

When we were babies, living in Alaska, I learned to crawl first. Pam hung on to my feet and let me drag her around from place to place. She did this for months until I got strong enough, and grew tired of her weight, to kick her a time or two. Only then did she start crawling on her own. Okay, maybe I need to rethink who the leader was in that situation.

I'll try again. As pre-teens in Douglasville, Georgia, I would encourage Pam . . . or dare her . . . to try things I was curious about, but was afraid to do . . . like shaving legs, wearing tampons, or using makeup. She wouldn't even hesitate. I would wait to see how our mom reacted and if she was okay with it, then it was clear sailing for me to do the same. When a boy called Pam in seventh grade, I sat at the kitchen table and studied my mom's reaction. She just smiled and handed Pam the phone. So, I knew that it would be okay to give Cleve, from my Social Studies Class, my phone number. Dad didn't pay attention to such things, leaving the approval decisions to Mom. And Mom was very trusting of us and generous in allowing Pam and me to grow with new pubescent experiences. Still, I was always the cautious one. I think this is a better example of my leadership skills.

I was happy to get back to my life in Georgia with my husband Dan, our mentally ill cat Roxie, and our rescue goldfish Judy, and put the whole nightmare behind me. Pam, on the other hand, wasn't done. She's a huge fan of the ID Channel and Forensics Files and so she answered every call from reporters and Hollywood folks who wanted to do a story on our adventure. Not me! I didn't know if the bad guys had vengeful relatives that might come after us. I just wanted to disappear into obscurity and peacefully cook quick, delicious meals for Dan in my microwave, write my children's plays, paint canvases on the back porch easel, and make pottery at the Blue Heron. I wanted to be left alone, but that wasn't going to happen. Not as long as Pam kept taking those calls.

CHAPTER 2
JENKEM
(Three Months Earlier)

Teg Duke walked out of Reston County Prison, a free man. Fifteen years inside had sallowed his skin and aged him more than any coke or booze could have ever done. The crime that sent Teg away wasn't drugs or alcohol related. It was an innocent little fling with a hot, cute girl. At least that's how he saw it. The prosecutor, the judge, and the jury saw it as sexual assault on a minor. The child was twelve, the daughter of Teg's pretend girlfriend, Eunice. Eunice wasn't much to look at and it killed Teg inside to have to sleep with her. She was big as a whale and had rotten teeth, and saggy tits. But, you do what you gotta do. Occasionally screwing Eunice was the only way he could get close to Amber.

Whenever the opportunity presented itself, when Eunice went shopping or to the hairdresser, Teg would have little dates with young Amber. That's how he thought of them, "dates." He started with sitting beside the pretty little brown haired girl and watching cartoons, sharing a bowl of ice cream or popcorn. Eventually, his hand would move to her leg and rest there. Then to her waistband. It was months before he got Amber to return the favors he bestowed on her. He never meant to go much further than oral sex. It was easy to keep that a secret . . . until it wasn't.

Teg couldn't believe the bitches had turned him in. After a memorable episode that went a lot further and was way more brutal than Teg had intended in the early stages of his "dating" the girl, Amber broke down crying at school. After some prodding, she told her teacher and the teacher, in turn, told Eunice and the police.

The woman judge . . . another bitch . . . sentenced him to twenty years, ten to serve. Most of his time was spent on Tier 3 because he was a sexual predator. Pedophiles, trans-genders, and rapists were sent to Tier 3 for their own protection. It grated on Teg to be lumped in with all the nut jobs. His current cellmate, Jimmy, was one of the he-shes, and Teg had come close to killing the weirdo squirrel a time or two. But he was smart enough to know that, however justified, murder would keep him in prison forever, and he wanted out.

With pretrial time served, Teg could have been out of there in ten, but trouble followed him during his stay. He had developed a hatred for one particular guard, Delvin Spencer, and that hatred had consequences. Teg saw right away that the guard had a stick up his ass. Officer Spencer was a foot short of being a midget and tried to make up for it by spending any off time at the gym, lifting weights to build up his tiny muscles. Teg could tell from his jaw line that he enhanced them with steroids, too. On top of that, he was an asshole who took his authority too far, daring defiance. All the inmates hated the little pumped up runt, but none more than Teg. And the feeling was mutual.

Spencer would smirk at Teg as he walked by his cell and would make comments like "You dreaming good tonight, Baby Raper?" Worse, he'd imply Teg was screwing Jimmy. And Teg was no homo. Spencer would say shit like "You girls quit playing with each other's pee pees and go to sleep." Or, "Jimmy's just your type Duke. Ain't you gotta thing for little girls?"

Another time, Spencer claimed Teg had spit at him. Teg had done no such thing. Spencer had been yelling up at him for dawdling on the yard. The whistle had sounded and Teg had been in no hurry to go back to his unair-conditioned cell. It was a beautiful day and a breeze was blowing, and so he'd taken his time. When Spencer stood on his tiptoes to try to scream in Teg's face to "Get a move on, Baby Raper," Teg had yelled a string of expletives right back. A little spittle flew out in the heat of the moment, but it wasn't intentional. Spencer called in reinforcements, and his lie caused Teg to spend three painful hours in a restraint chair with a mesh spit hood over his face.

Teg bided his time. A week later, he was standing in line for chow when Spencer walked by him and made a sound like he was hawking up a loogie. Teg wasn't sure if Spencer was going to spit a wad at him in retaliation, or if he had made the sound to frame him again. Didn't matter. One good punch in the jaw to the little piss ant corrections officer, followed by a write up, followed by another court hearing, and Teg was assigned two years in solitary in a hole they called the "Shoe." That should have been enough to make him walk the straight and narrow. But of course it wasn't, and Teg actually liked the Shoe . . . liked having a cell to himself.

That night, the night of the Jenkem, Teg took note that Delvin Spencer was on duty and would be overseeing his tier. Staffing at night had been short lately, and there was a good chance that he could pull off a Jenkem on old Delvin. The son of a bitch was still provoking Teg . . . ordering him around . . . tossing his cell for imagined contraband . . . pushing him against the wall extra hard during a body search. Most of all, he knew Spencer was behind transferring Jimmy back to his house after his time in the Shoe, just so he could continue his taunting.

Like other long stint prisoners, Teg liked to refer to his cell as his "house." Why not? It's where he lived . . . at least for now. He made sure Jimmy knew that it wasn't HIS house and the girly squirrel sure wasn't Teg's guest. Jimmy was a diseased, interloping rat that needed to be trapped and poisoned, and Teg had said as much to his cellmate. Jimmy would just laugh at him, too crazy to feel threatened.

Jimmy was always getting himself sent to the psych ward by doing idiotic stuff like sticking a pencil up his pee hole. He'd save up food from his tray to smoosh and rub on his skin like it was girl's makeup. One day, Jimmy had peanut butter eyelids and he hung over his bunk and fluttered them at Teg. Teg couldn't stand him, but he hated the guard worse. Tonight would take care of both problems because he knew he'd be back in the Shoe for a long, long time. It was worth it. He preferred solitary.

Teg lay on his bunk and watched Jimmy doing little sissy leg lifts on the cold concrete floor. Jimmy would squeal "Ouchy" in his annoying high-pitched voice after each and every lift. Jimmy did this routine every night before bed. Tonight, Teg said nothing.

He knew Jimmy would finish and climb in his bunk and go to sleep.

Finally, Teg heard Jimmy snoring from the bunk above. He reached behind the toilet and pulled out a plastic bag. He'd been saving his piss and shit for days and had let it cook up nicely in the garbage bag. The fermented mixture was known as "Jenkem" amongst prisoners and considered a lethal weapon by the guards. Some cons even added their blood to nasty up the concoction even more. Teg just stuck to the basics.

Teg opened the bag, gagging on the foul odor. It took a minute or two before he could continue. He knew it was easier to get used to your own stink than someone else's. So it wasn't long before he was able to take a deep breath and put his mouth over the opening of the bag. Teg blew enough air to make a good sized balloon, and then wiped his mouth and tied off the bag. He waited by the bars, a patient man.

Around midnight, Teg heard footsteps coming down the tier. It was a rare quiet night. Usually, men were crying, hollering, singing, cussing, or carrying on late into the night. But not tonight. This night, the cons were surprisingly settled. It was gonna be a great night on Tier 3.

Delvin Spencer had his flashlight out looking into each cell. He was delighted that nothing was going on for once and, just maybe, he and the other guards could spend the remaining seven hours of their shift playing some gin rummy or cribbage in the office. His shoulder mic crackled with officer Burton reporting that Tier 2 was clear and all inmates were bunked in. This was followed by officer Parham reporting an all clear for Tier 1. He'd be making the same report shortly.

A shadow from the last cell stopped Spencer and caused him to twitch. A tingling chill ran down his back, clinching his sphincter. He knew it was Teg's house. The prisoner had broken his jaw two years back and he would never forget the pain. His jaw had been wired for weeks, and he'd dropped ten pounds of muscle mass eating pureed food through a straw. On cold days, the jaw still ached.

Spencer stepped forward to the edge of the cell.

"Who's up in there? Lights out faggots. Get in your bunks."

No sound. He took another step, shining the flashlight up and down. And another step.

Then, from within the cell, he heard, "Eat my shit you little piss ant!"

And with that statement, Teg hurled the Jenkem at Spencer. Bullseye! The bag exploded right in the officer's face. Teg jumped back to avoid the overspray. The officer screamed, clawing at his eyes and mouth.

"That'll teach ya to open your big mouth. Taste good to you piss ant?"

Spencer fell to the floor, writhing and yelling. His cries were inhuman . . . guttural. And with each scream, more of the pickled fecal juice ran into his mouth, up his nose, and in his eyes.

Jimmy sat up in his bunk and squealed in his little girl voice. "Oooo . . . Look what you did!"

Feet running down the hall . . . Officers with helmets, shields and pepper spray signaled an end to Teg's fun. He was ready for the Shoe and a happy, happy man.

And, he did go to the Shoe. But, that wasn't all. The attack lengthened his stay an extra five years, and that really pissed him off. Nobody cared that he was only defending himself . . . that he was justified. Nothing he could do about it, and it didn't matter. He was out now. And he was hungry. Hungry as a man could be hungry. But not for food.

CHAPTER 3
A HORRIBLE DEATH

My microwave is dead. I found out from a note written on a napkin by my husband and left on the living room ottoman at the foot of my favorite chair. That is exactly what the note said, "*MICROWAVE IS DEAD.*" Nice way to start my morning. This was a full year after the grisly adventure with Pam, and it is just the type of case I'm more comfortable solving. I didn't have to call in a forensics team to help with this one. I knew who killed my microwave. I've warned Dan over and over to put plastic wrap over stuff he nukes. But does he listen? No!

Just to be sure, I went to the kitchen and put a cup of water inside the microwave. I wasn't sure what the water was for, but I've always heard you were supposed to do that if you had nothing to cook. I looked over at my pristine, hardly used stove and prayed. "Please, Jesus, with all your majestic angels sitting on big, thick, fluffy clouds playing on golden harpsichords, don't let my microwave be dead. And, please don't make me have to cook on that stove with pots and pans. Amen." That task done, I hit the quick start button putting a minute on the timer, and pressed the larger start button. Nothing. I wiggled the plug. Nothing. I unplugged it and waited ten minutes before re-plugging, like we do when the cable goes out. Nothing.

I called Pam to tell her about this horror. My twin was less than sympathetic.

"Dan didn't kill your microwave. It died from overuse and abuse. If you would cook on a stove like a real person, you would find that your food actually has flavor."

Pam is so judgmental.

I put in a call to POLLOCK'S APPLIANCE AND MUSICAL INSTRUMENT REPAIR over on Cedar Street. Neil Pollock arrived with his red and rusty tool box later in the afternoon.

He examined my microwave making little tsk-tsk mutterings as he worked.

"Somebody heat left over spaghetti in this appliance without covering the dish with plastic wrap?"

"Yes. That would be my husband."

Neil reached in his toolbox without looking and pulled out a tool that looked like a staple remover to snag the little pin that holds the waveguide cover in place.

"How about Chicken pot pie?"

I felt very defensive. "That would also be Dan."

More tsk tsking and muttering, as he removed the waveguide cover and shined a pin light.

"You know folks think the microwave was invented in World War II by the Army."

"I've heard that."

"Yeah, well. They're wrong."

"You don't say."

Neil had a wire brush that he inserted into the waveguide opening and began making little circular motions. The man is a genius with appliances and musical instruments.

"Evidence shows it was first carried in the Ark of the Covenant thousands of years ago, and it was used as a lethal weapon."

"The Ark of the . . . You mean in the Bible? Did they have electricity back then?"

He ignored my question and replaced the wire brush with a long dowel covered in lambskin. I seemed to remember that same tool, years ago when he fixed my son Chris' trumpet.

He quoted, "*It glowed in the dark, made whirling noises, and killed everyone that laid hands on it* . . . Sounds familiar don't it?"

"I see your point." I was amused and oddly, almost convinced.

"I believe that if the Ark is found today, we will see written in ancient Hebrew, the name *Amanna* . . . The Jews ate Manna . . . I'm just sayin' . . . ."

I didn't know if he was pulling my leg, but I was highly entertained. Sadly, after an hour of trying, Neil pronounced my Microwave as most sincerely dead. Whatever an inverter is, mine had shorted out, and it would cost about the same to repair as to buy new. There would be no second coming.

And that's what led me to the place of my nightmares . . . the place to which I had sworn I'd never return . . . The Carrollton Walmart.

CHAPTER 4
FREEDOM
(Three months earlier)

Teg's freedom had some restrictions. He didn't mind most of them. He walked into the Dekalb County halfway house and met with Darnell, the house manager. All he had in his pocket was his comb, his wallet and the $45 given to him at the prison when he processed out. Teg refused to take the prison-issued free sweat suit he was offered. The clothes he was wearing were the same clothes he'd arrived at the prison with fifteen years before. They had been stored in a zip lock bag all that time, along with the wallet and comb. He'd be throwing them away as soon as he had some real money.

There were forms to fill out.

Full Name: Thomas Granger Duke
AKA: Teg Duke
Age: 37
Height: 6'2"
Weight: 220
Hair Color: Brown
Eye Color: Brown
Tattoos (Location and Description):

Darnell filled this part out with a required strip inspection of his client. He had seen some of these before, and when he knew it, he added their meaning. There was no color in any of them. This was typical with prison tattoos. Darnell labeled them all black, but some, with time and fading, had actually turned a greenish color.

1. Left Shoulder – Spider Web – Black
2. Under left eye – 3 dots – Black – (The three dots tattoo represents "mi vida loca," or "my crazy life.")

3. Right Elbow – 88 – Black – (8ᵗʰ letter of the Alphabet. HH for Heil Hitler)
4. Top of back beneath neck – bird flying – Black – (May be a symbol for freedom or desire for freedom – not sure.)
5. Back Center – Face of a girl. – Black – (Don't know who. Client says it is random.)

Right hand fingers – numbers on each of four fingers starting with pinky: 1, 4, 8, 8 – Black – (White supremacist numbers – 14 represents 14 words from a quote by Nazi leader David Lane: "We must secure the existence of our people and a future for White Children." 88 is a repeat of the Heil Hitler symbol.

This part of the form completed, Darnell allowed Teg to dress. He filled in the rest of the information on the form like social security number, parole requirements, and last home address. Teg gave his father's Cabbage Town address, the same old house on the outskirts of Atlanta that he'd grown up in. The bottom portion of the form would wait until Teg had registered as a sex offender, secured ID, and received his outside job assignment.

Teg looked at the house manager, at the dread locks that covered his head. He didn't like to have to answer to black folks, but he had no choice. He'd have to do whatever it took to stay free.

Darnell drove Teg to the Atlanta DMV. Teg was issued a state ID, not a driver's license. He would have to earn that privilege later. With the ID in his pocket, Teg walked into the warehouse, Darnell at his side. He met with the manager and got his shift assignment. The warehouse manager, a balding, portly white man in his forties, was delighted to have a big, muscular man to lift the heavy boxes from the fork lift. Last dude they'd sent him had been a scrawny crack addict and hadn't lasted the week. This guy would do.

Teg liked the halfway house. He liked his room with the twin bed with a real mattress, the three drawer chest with a mirror above, and the air conditioner in the window. And, he liked his job. He walked the mile and a half back and forth to work every day unless it rained. On rainy days Darnell drove him to work and picked him up. Teg preferred to walk. First of all, he loved being outdoors and second of all, he didn't like folks seeing him in a car with a black man. But mostly, he liked walking by the schoolyard and seeing children, especially the little girls.

CHAPTER 5
BIG BOX SHOP OF HORRORS

I pulled into the Walmart parking lot and parked in the only open space I could find. Thankfully, the rain had stopped. I opened my door halfway, so as not to hit the man leaning against the passenger side of the huge truck on giant tractor wheels parked next to me. He was wearing a baseball cap with a rebel flag on the front. As I sidled past him, he spit tobacco juice and the spittle landed right on the top of my sandaled foot.

I stopped and glared at him and said, "Nice. Really?"

He looked at me with a chaw of tobacco the size of a grapefruit in his jaw, "Hey lady, I spit before you walked. Ain't my fault you put yore foot where I was spittin'!"

They had some handi-wipes at the front door for moms to clean off the shopping cart handles so their little tots could gnaw on them. I took about five of them and ignored the Greeter Lady as I cleaned off my foot. That task completed, I made my way into the merchandise jungle.

I tried to find the appliance section . . . Lord knows where that is! . . . But, I got distracted by a sales table special on pillowcases. There were stacks and stacks of them in every color imaginable. I could always use burgundy pillowcases in regular sizes. These, however, seemed to be all king sized and I had plenty of those. You couldn't tell the size without unfolding them . . . and then, of course, you needed to refold them because people were watching . . . Lots of beige regular sized, so maybe I should just switch colors altogether. Of course, if I did go this route, I'd need new sheets to match and they probably weren't on sale. If I took the plunge, I could go a whole other color since I really hated beige, but that would require a new comforter and duvet. Oh, and throw pillows . . . This was how Walmart got you. I was totally consumed in deep bedding thoughts when the man walked up behind me.

"Excuse me, Ma'am."

I jumped a little and dropped the green 300 count pillowcase with satin edging I was refolding.

"Hello?" I was wary.

He was in his early thirties, handsome, blondish and tall, but haggard. Very haggard.

"Aren't you that lady from the papers that solved that murder in Tennessee last year?"

I'm sure I looked wary, but I nodded. "We didn't solve it on purpose. It was . . ."

He cut me off. "Can you help me find my daughter?" He handed me a small picture, printed off a computer of a pretty young blonde child of about seven or eight.

I felt very sympathetic. "She's lovely. But, you do know I'm not a detective. The stuff you read in the paper about my cousin . . . it just sort of happened. I'm an artist and my sister, she's a retired school teacher."

"You and your sister, you made that happen. You solved the case. My little girl has been missing for almost a week. Please, just take this with you and think on it. She's only six. My number is on the back."

And with that, he walked away. I flipped the piece of paper over and saw he had written *Leman Garrett* and a phone number. Under that was, I presume, the little girl's name, *Cara Louise Garrett*. Six? The little blonde child seemed older . . . wiser somehow.

I stuck the paper in my pocket. I felt bad for the guy. I really did. But, I'm not a detective. He needed to take advantage of our wonderful local police if he wanted an investigation. What did he expect me to do about it?

I caressed the pillowcases, promising them to return later and went in search of appliances. I would have asked for help, but I do indeed like solving mysteries . . . like Sudoku puzzles . . . not murders . . . not child disappearances. After about twenty minutes of circling the same aisles, I finally stumbled on the correct one.

I picked out the fanciest, biggest stainless steel microwave with all the bells and whistles Walmart had. Problem was I forgot to get a shopping buggy, and so, I would have to lug the big heavy box with the new Panasonic microwave with rotating carousel and convection fan, whatever that was, to the checkout line. Going for a buggy first was out of the question as I didn't have bread crumbs to drop to find my way back, and that is probably frowned on by staff, anyway. So I set the huge box on the floor and pushed it with my foot, all the way to the register line.

Miraculously, I headed in the right direction. I think my menopausal body was drawn to the cool outside air near the entrance. Hot flashes will seek out a breeze, any breeze. Sometimes that's useful when you are lost. There were about a dozen checkout lines, but only one was lit up and so I had to stand behind six other people with my microwave on the floor. I didn't mind as my back needed the break. I wondered how I would ever get this box to the car and up and in the back of the Trail Blazer.

Thankfully, a young pimply faced teenager with a blue vest and a walkie talkie helped me get the microwave to my car and loaded. He accepted my tip with a smile and a thanks, but refused to follow me home to unload the box. It would just have to wait for Dan to get home from work.

CHAPTER 6
CARA'S JOURNAL AND SKETCHBOOK
(One Week Earlier)

I wore my pink Tinkerbell pajamas to bed last night. Theyre my favorite, even more than the pink Pretty Pretty Pony ones in the bottom drawer. My Gramma sent me these for Christmas. She lives up in Nebraska and Daddy says I can visit her sometime when its warmer.

My pajama top has my name on the front with pink thread. It says Cara. Most people spell Cara with a K and I cant ever find anything with my name on it which just isnt fair at all. Gramma spelled it right though. I sure wish I had a tag for my bicycle that says Cara. But the stores only have the ones that say Kara. Daddy says he will make me one. Hes been looking for a tag that says Lara cause he says that will be easier to paint over than Kara. My Daddy is very smart. He nos things.

My Daddy is taking me on a picnic today. He says its the only chance we have before the rain comes tonight. The pretty Weatherman girl says theres gonna be days and days of rain. So just in case I might wear my rain boots.

Im going to wear my jeans and sparkley pink shirt. Pink is my favorit color in case you cant tell that.

Daddy made me some bacon and eggs and a cut up orange. This orange doesnt have any seeds in it. Can you beleve it?

Daddy says my rain boots are just fine cause we are going to the Little Talapusa River for our picnic and I can use them to wade if I stay close to the edge. But he says it wont rain until we get back. I wish my Mommy could come with us. But she cant because she died. That makes me sad.

CHAPTER 7
COOKING UP A PLOT

Dan arrived home from the university around six and ate his Zaxby's salad. I couldn't cook without a microwave, obviously, and had picked up dinner. Later, I sat on a stool on the screened porch and worked on an oil painting while Dan lugged the new appliance from my car into the kitchen. He joined me on the porch and handed me a gin and tonic. He squeezed lime into his own glass and sipped it as we chatted.

"We have a problem. You bought a bigger microwave than the one we had."

"So?" I used a fan brush to wisp some clouds over the Blue Ridge Mountains, looking at a photograph I had taken from my brother's back deck.

"So . . . it won't fit under the cabinet. You'll have to return it."

"If I return it, I will have to buy pillowcases and a new comforter. I can't go back there."

Dan swirled the ice in his drink and nodded. He did not ask me to explain. He was probably thinking this was a symptom of my menopause, but he wisely thought better of saying so. He'd learned not to confront me on these episodes. But I'd noticed lately, he was fixing my drinks with more ice than usual.

"Do you have a plan, then? It's hanging halfway over into the sink."

"I do. Just leave it where it is for now. I'll fix it. Tell me about your day."

And that was that.

The next morning, Pam called. I knew she would and had my phone in the pocket of my jeans.

"Hey, whatcha doing?" she asked.

"Lying on my back on the kitchen counter, chiseling the bottom of the spice cabinet."

"What for?" I could hear her sipping coffee.

"So the new microwave will fit."

"Why don't you return it and buy a smaller one?"

I sat up to explain, smashing my head into the cabinet above. Pam waited patiently, enjoying her coffee, while I grabbed a cold wet dishtowel to speed up the coagulation.

My head pounded and I was seeing stars. I went on to explain about the pillowcases. Pam fully understood this. She's been to those big box stores herself. She even has a Sam's membership. So, she knows how they suck you in.

I also told her about my encounter with Leman Garrett.

"Did you tell Dan? What did he say?"

"He said something like, 'Don't you dare call that man.' . . . Or something like that. I didn't mind. It was a distraction from explaining about the pillowcases."

"I still get weird phone calls from people, too, now and then, since we got back. A lady keeps calling me wanting me to give her lottery numbers. She called again last night."

"Lord. What did you tell her?"

"I told her 7, 14, 22, 89, 93 and Powerball 5."

"Really, Pam? You told her that? Were you right?" I rinsed the blood out of my dishrag and added an ice cube.

"Nope. So, she'll probably leave me alone, now."

We chatted awhile and I felt myself drifting off. I probably had a concussion. I'm prone to them in the kitchen.

The cabinet would need to wait awhile as my head hurt something awful. Thankfully, a Goody's Powder poured right onto my tongue and an hour long nap perked me right up, the pain gone. I looked at the clock. 3:00 p.m.

I knew I would have to start dinner soon using the pristine stove that came with our house when we bought it twenty years ago. This problem had reached a critical point as my sweet little ninety-two-year-old mother-in-law, Nancy . . . Nannee to the grandchildren . . . was supposed to help me bake cookies later in the week. Those recipes of hers always include softened butter, and how in the world does one soften butter without a microwave?

The cord wouldn't reach the outlet where it sat now, so my new appliance was unusable until I could get it to fit properly. Dan frowned on my use of extension cords. He has good reason, but that's another story. What to cook? I was perplexed.

I dug around in the freezer, looking sadly at the frozen Stouffers Lasagna with Meat Sauce with the reflective box that allows you to cook it in a microwave in 12-13 minutes by folding the box magically into a reflective tray. Temptation to stick it in the stove's oven hovered, but I wasn't sure the plastic dish would hold up.

I found some hamburger meat in the back of the freezer and had this inspiration that I could make my own lasagna from scratch like other people do. I set the hamburger outside by the pool thinking the sun would do the thawing and I could make a nice homemade pan that would blow Dan's socks off. Normally, of course, I thaw stuff in my microwave on the number 3 setting.

I didn't have ricotta cheese for the inside layer, but I did have a six-pack of yogurt sized cottage cheeses that I could substitute. I peeled back their little covers and dumped the cheese into a bowl. I stirred in a couple of eggs and set it aside for later. Digging again in the freezer, I found a Ziploc bag of mozzarella. I was in business.

I put on the reading glasses I keep in the kitchen and pulled out a box of pasta from the pantry. The directions on the back said, 1) In a 6-8 quart stock pot, over high heat, bring 4-6 quarts of water to a rolling boil. Add salt. 2) Add desired amount of pasta to boiling water. Stir gently. Return to boil. 3) Boil uncovered, stirring occasionally, 8-9 minutes for "al dente" pasta. 4. Drain.

The directions were easy enough and I had other stuff to do, and so, I thought it would be totally reasonable to skip a step or two. I filled my big pot with cold water, turned the stove knob to high and went ahead and tossed in the pasta. The stiff uncooked pasta stood straight up in the pan about six inches above the water. I figured it could just wait right there for the water to come to a boil. The pasta would eventually soften and sink into the pan.

I returned to my painting on the porch, which desperately needed a little raw umber on the edges of the tree limbs. I made a mental note to myself that I should check the pasta in about ten minutes or so.

Frowning at the landscape, I just wasn't happy with it. It was a pleasant enough painting, but it was no different from the last twenty I had done. Boring. I tilted my head sideways and studied the canvas. I had an urge to tilt the painting the same way as my neck, and I did just that. I turned the painting vertical on the easel so that the branches of the trees fell to the right, and was struck at how something dramatic and peculiar hovered, waiting to be revealed. The mountains now sloped downward, curving like a body. The tree branches, like hair.

I dabbed a bit of crimson into the white on my pallet creating a soft pink. The same crimson mixed with the sky blue became lavender. I mixed some greens. I moved the paint in a flowing manner to cover some of the brown tree bark but left the twisted hair-like branches. A ghostly image of a young girl in a pretty green dress began to appear. A stony blue river soon became a pink ribbon flowing through curly tresses. I painted her from behind. I didn't want to show her face, but I did want to capture something magical and spritely. Her arm lifted to the lower branch of the one tree that remained . . . holding on . . . waiting for rescue.

Somewhere I had those sparkling gold pieces that I had forged at my friend Joel's studio that could be adhered with a little gesso right to the painting. I wanted to weave them into the hair around the ribbon and on in to the sky above. I knew they were somewhere in my storage box. But where?

A couple of hours later, I heard the fire alarm. Dang it. I'd forgotten the stove. The house was full of smoke, but it wasn't just the burnt dry pot and crispy black pasta. I'd left my reading glasses a little too close to the stove eye. They were melted all over the glass top burner. And they were my favorite glasses, too. The pair I used outside had paint flecks crusted in the hinges and I rarely wore them in public. I may have to go back to Walmart, after all.

I turned off the stove, grabbed the pot, and put it in the sink. I ran cold water and had to jump back from the putrid steam that hit me in the face. My elbow hit the bowl of cottage cheese, knocking it to the floor. White curds, raw eggs, and pottery shards scattered in every conceivable direction. I left the mess there and opened doors to clear out the smoke.

When I got to the screen door that led to the porch, I saw our cat, Roxie, rolled over on her back on the pool deck, munching on my now thawed hamburger meat. The ripped, bloody cellophane was between her paws, and she wore the happiest expression I'd ever seen on that cat's face. Pieces of the white Styrofoam tray were floating in the pool.

Plan B. I called James Gross at La Trattoria's in Adamson Square and ordered lasagna to go. I would transfer their dish to my dish and Dan would be none the wiser. I changed clothes, threw on some lipstick, and drove the three miles into town.

I chatted with James for a bit while I paid for my order. We've been friends for years and I knew he wouldn't tell on me.

James handed me my to-go bag. "Are you sure you wouldn't rather have Eggplant Parmesan? You know Dan loves my Eggplant."

"Now James, you know he'll know if I do that. And he never orders your lasagna."

As I headed for the door, I stopped to read the fliers posted on the big picture window. There was a large one for the upcoming Carroll County Community Theatre production of "I'm Not Rappaport," a smaller flier for the Community Chorus Holiday show and several for upcoming free music concerts at the Amphitheatre. And off to one side, there was an 8x12 sheet of paper with a picture of the little missing girl, Cara Louise Garrett. The picture was clearer than the one in my purse, and I could see curly blonde tresses and her sparkly eyes shimmering with life and love. I felt very sad and very curious.

Back home, I used a razor blade to scrape the cooled plastic reading glasses from the stove top and threw them away with the ruined pot, burying both deep in the outside garbage can. The black lasagna noodles, I stuffed into a plastic grocery bag. They had sort of melded together into one big thick pasta brick. For one short moment, I contemplated using them as a sculpture medium. But they smelled so bad I just couldn't. I forced myself to throw them away, too . . . deep in the can . . . like the burnt pot and my glasses. I crawled on my knees and swept up the cottage cheese, eggs, and pottery shards with a combination of dustpan and wet rag. I rinsed out the rag and cleaned the gunk off the chair legs and out of the heat vent. Finally, I sprayed the whole house with Febreeze and turned on all the ceiling fans.

Smoke and blackened utensils disposed of, I transferred the La Trattoria lasagna into my nice cut glass casserole dish and made a salad. As a bonus surprise, I made some garlic bread from leftover hotdog buns, cooking them in the toaster oven. I set the table with the good china, tossed a salad, and lit some scented candles. This was going to be great!

CHAPTER 8
DINNER WITH DAN

Dan was thrilled. We toasted each other with Red Rock Malbec over a candlelit dinner at our little kitchen table. He was a happy man, even having seconds of the scrumptious lasagna. We talked about our day and I told him I was working on a new painting. Then, I kind of slipped up a little.

"I saw a flier today on that missing little girl. So sad."

"Where did you see it?" His mouth was full of pasta and garlic bread.

"Er umm. Somewhere not sure . . ."

"Was it on the picture window at La Trattoria's when you picked up this lasagna?"

Dang this man! I laid down my fork and looked at him.

"What gave me away?"

"The receipt is lying out there on the garage floor."

He didn't mind, though. He knew I'd been through a lot of stress lately. And the dinner was wonderful and romantic. Dan's always happy when he eats well.

CHAPTER 9
PICNIC ALONG THE RIVER
(One Week Earlier)

Cara and her daddy spread a blanket near the river's edge. They had carried their picnic fixins in plastic grocery bags. Leman let Cara set it all out. Paper plates, peanut butter and jelly sandwiches, an orange for Cara and a banana for Leman, and little bags of chips. Another bag held a small Ziploc of ice and a thermos of Kool-Aid. Cara carefully dealt out the ice cubes evenly into the two plastic solo cups and with her Dad's watchful eye, she carefully poured the drink.

"Look at you all grown up. You didn't spill a drop."

Cara beamed. She sat up straighter and put the lid on the remaining Kool-Aid and carefully set it aside.

"Daddy, this place is so pretty."

"It is. See the river flowing over those rocks near the edge?"

"Yes, sir."

"We have a lot of rain coming. By next week, you won't be able to see those rocks like you can now. Not even the big ones. The river will be a lot deeper."

"I don't see rocks in the middle of the river. How come?"

"It's already deep out there, and the river will rise even more. Would you like to come back in a couple of weeks and see how it's changed?"

Cara smiled with delight. "Yes, Daddy. Let's do that."

They ate their lunch on the riverbank, watching the view and the creatures of the wood. A large frog hopped from rock to rock before plunging into the swiftly flowing river. Angry grey clouds were starting to form in the blue sky above. They had a few hours still to enjoy. Lunch finished, Cara helped clean up, and then, pulled out her sketchpad and colored pencils from her backpack. Leman lay on his back and watched her as she sketched the view. For a little girl, she had a steady hand, an artistic soul, and a gift for drawing.

Cara had the same blonde hair as her mother. It was curlier but held the same natural highlights of varying shades. Julie never dyed her hair. She didn't need to. Other women would often ask her for the name of her hairdresser. They couldn't believe it was real.

Leman and Julie had met in college at the University of West Georgia. He was a business major, Julie, art. Like their daughter was becoming, Julie was a gifted artist. Her oil paintings hung throughout the home. Julie might be gone these four years, but her paintings helped keep her present and inspired Cara's own creativity. As he walked through the house, Leman liked to touch the paintings softly along the ridges of the brush strokes. He could close his eyes and imagine his love's hand moving so gently on the canvas, on his skin, over his body.

A year after their marriage, Julie was diagnosed with Ovarian Cancer. The big C. She rejected the prescribed hysterectomy which would end her chance for motherhood, opting instead for chemo and radiation. Leman took on an extra job at night, stocking shelves at Kroger to help cover the costs for treatment not covered by insurance. In the daytime, Leman worked at a medical billing office, long hours filing forms and typing emails to doctors' offices.

Leman insisted that Julie quit teaching art at the local elementary school and stay home to heal and to paint. She missed the children, but the treatments were exhausting and so, she agreed. He turned the guest room into a studio for her. The studio would later become Cara's bedroom.

Six months into treatment, Julie found out she was expecting a baby, despite the precautions the couple had taken. Leman never mentioned, but always suspected, that the pregnancy might have been on purpose. The medical team wanted to abort, but Julie refused. Leman asked her to reconsider. They could have another child, and he was scared she was making a mistake. He begged her to listen to the experts. And to make matters worse, Julie stopped the chemo. These were her decisions to make. She promised to start back once the baby was born, but it was too late. The Cancer spread, and Julie died when Cara was two.

Little Cara had no memory of her beautiful mother and that pained Leman greatly. Occasionally, Cara would ask questions, and Leman would show her pictures and tell her of exaggerated grand adventures that the couple had experienced. Their time together was too short, and too filled with sickness to have had any true adventures. So Leman made up stories, including whimsical talking animals met at the top of majestic mountains, castles with princesses and knights in shining armor, and dragons, and sometimes visits in the starry night from fairies like Tinkerbell.

Her daddy's stories inspired Cara to write her own, just as her mother's paintings inspired her artwork. Even in Kindergarten, she could write words, far beyond the expectations of her teacher.

A few weeks before, a teary-eyed Cara asked her daddy if she would ever get to see her mommy. He took her little head in his hands and turned her toward the bathroom mirror. "Look, Cara. Look in the mirror anytime you want to see your mother. You look just like her."

Cara turned and hugged her daddy hard and then turned back to the mirror, peering hard at her reflection. "I'm so glad, Daddy." She smiled. "I'm so glad I can see her."

Leman loved to watch Cara draw. He loved this quiet connection to his daughter and her gentle ways, so much like his Julie's. Also like Julie, Cara was smart. Smarter than he would ever be. A very good speller . . . not perfect . . . but very good for a first grader, she liked to write as much as she liked to draw. If a word was too big, she tried anyway, and he could always figure out what she meant. There was a richness and maturity to her words.

He had noticed that she had started using her sketchpad as a sort of journal in between the pictures. Leman wasn't one to pry, but sometimes at night, he would sit on the edge of her bed, beside his magical, sleeping child. He would flip through her sketch pad, illuminated by a nightlight, marveling at the detail in the drawings.

And then on another page or between the drawings, he would read her sweet words, so advanced for her age.

Sometimes Cara would write about the little daily details of her life–karate class, school, church, and friends. Sometimes, she wrote about her mother, an angel she didn't really know, but imagined. And sometimes, she wrote about him. Her love permeated the pages and made him want to grab her up and hug her. Of course, he didn't. He would let her sleep. Leman looked forward to reading what she would write about their picnic.

Leman couldn't be prouder of his little girl, and he told her so. Cara smiled and said, "Well, I'm proud of you, too, Daddy." The sounds of Cara's sketching were rhythmic and soon he felt his eyelids grow heavy. He drifted off to a dreamless sleep.

Cara didn't mind at all. She enjoyed the occasional sight of a little animal from the woods running up a tree or across the river bank, the rustle of the leaves from the drifting breeze, and the babbling rising river. Most of all, she loved sitting next to her daddy. Cara smiled again at her sleeping father and turned back to her work. A squirrel sat very still in front of her, an acorn in its paws. The squirrel was frozen, as if in pose, like a model. Deeply focused, Cara quietly began sketching an outline of the animal and soon became lost in her drawing.

CHAPTER 10
FAVORS

I got up early the next morning and went back to work, chiseling under the cabinet. Around ten o'clock, I got frustrated and, rubbing my sore shoulder, I quit, and went in search of Ben Gay. The bathroom closet door was already partially open, and I found Roxie's sleeping place choice of the day.

Our cat rarely sleeps in the same spot more than a couple of times. The week before, she spent two days in the potato basket, and three days stretched on the rim of our bathtub. Her weekend bedroom was Dan's closet, curled above his shoe rack, balanced on his Cole Hahns. There must be some leonine protection defense deep in her DNA that causes her to change locations frequently. That I understand, but still, Dan and I found some of Roxie's choices to be odd.

Today, she was in the bathroom closet on top of the bucket of cleaning supplies, draped over a can of Comet and a bottle of Windex. The spray nozzle of the window cleaner dug deep into her gut. Beside the bucket was a nice patch of soft carpeting. Why she would choose such an uncomfortable spot was beyond my understanding. My pottery teacher, Melanie Drew, once suggested that maybe it was kitty yoga. Whatever it was, it was weird.

I found the Ben Gay on the top shelf and, rubbing the ointment into my arm, I called Pam.

"Could you drive down here and exchange my microwave for me? I need a smaller one."

"I will do no such thing."

"Why? I'm desperate."

"Like you, I avoid that place."

"You could make an exception just this once."

"No. I can't. I'm a teacher."

"You are a retired teacher."

"Doesn't matter. When teachers go to Walmart, every kid we ever taught and their mothers are there. We see them looking in our buggies at our beer, tampons, and Monistat 7."

"So what? You taught the blind."

"They judge us. Instead of focusing on little Johnny's grades at the next teacher conference, they are looking at me like I'm some PMS-ing drunk with vaginal itch."

"Is this a for real problem? I mean, I repeat, YOU TAUGHT THE BLIND. They can't see in your cart."

"Their parents can. It's why I drive to Alabama to buy beer."

Plan B. I called my friend Lizzie Barganier.

"Hey, Lizzie. Need a favor."

"I'm not exchanging your microwave for you."

"What? How did you . . . Pam called you didn't she? She couldn't have called you that quick."

"She sent me a Facebook Chat message while you were talking to her on the phone. She knew I'd be next on your list. And I'm not doing it. I love you, but, you need to face your own demons."

I went back to my chiseling. A bit of anger added force to my efforts. Finally, around four o'clock, I slid the new microwave right into place. Letting out a loud whoop, I felt such relief and pride at my accomplishment. With great flourish, I plugged it in and used the beverage setting to reheat a cup of coffee.

I badly needed a heating pad, some more muscle rub, and a White Russian over chipped ice. I settled for the coffee. I would add a little trim to the bottom of the cabinet the next day to cover up the numerous scratch marks. Or maybe I would just find a brown Sharpie marker in my tool box or makeup bag. Sharpies are part of my arsenal. I even use a black one to touch up my roots and eyebrows.

I was too pooped to work on my painting so I stretched out on the couch with my coffee, a mirror, and a black Sharpie, and called my mother.

"Hey, Mom." I had her on speaker so that I could Sharpie my hairline.

"Hey, Penny." Folks think Pam and I sound exactly alike. Our mom always knows the difference immediately.

"You still angry at me and Pam? Sherry called me the other day and said you were still mad."

Sherry is my first cousin and lives fairly close to Mom. "It's been almost a year, Mom."

I knew she wasn't mad. My mother loves to rehash stuff and, in celebration of the morning's achievement, I felt like generously indulging her.

"Now you know I'm not. You girls scared me half to death with your shenanigans up in Athens. You could have been killed and poor Dan . . . What he must have gone through . . ."

"Dan played golf the whole time we were gone. I don't think he suffered much." I flicked a piece of sawdust out of my coffee and lightly feathered my eyebrows with the Sharpie.

Mom began reciting the entire event in Tennessee, including the part where Pam and I were cowering in smelly coats in a closet with murderers hovering over us. She told the story as if I hadn't been there and knew it all first hand. We refer to her repeated tales as "corn stories."

The phrase "corn story" goes back about thirty years to my maternal Grandmother. She had bought a pile of corn on the cobb at a real cheap price at the grocery store. Turns out they had been mismarked, but the nice grocer had let her buy them for a nickel a piece anyway. Everyone else that came into the store had to pay a quarter an ear. Granny had cooked up the whole mess and brought it to the family reunion. As each family member arrived, they had to hear the whole corn story. By the time we left, we had heard it told about twenty-five times.

Mom had just finished the closet story and had moved on to Pam's assault in the Microtel. Her voice was getting increasingly loud. I just sipped my coffee, touched up the grey at my temple, and let her go. Finally, she said, "Let's just change the subject. My stomach can't take any more stress today."

"Good idea. Nancy's coming over on Saturday to help me with baking. I need your good chocolate chip cookie recipe. The one where the cookies are flat but stay chewy."

"You're going to bake?"

I don't know why my family is shocked when I cook something. "Yes, Mom . . . with Nancy."

"Oh, thank goodness, someone will be there to supervise you. Please tell that sweet lady hello from me."

My mother and my mother-in-law adore one another.

"I hope you still have that Silvadene burn cream I gave you last year. Do you have a pencil? Make sure you use White Lily flour. If you don't, there's just no point making them." Mom dictated the recipe from memory.

CHAPTER 11
GOOD FRIENDS
(Two Months Earlier)

Teg hated to admit it, but he was actually beginning to like Darnell. For a black man, Darnell was cool. Angus would have a fit if he saw his son hanging with a black man. Teg's daddy didn't cotton to such things.

Darnell would pop popcorn and bring it into the common room that the ex-cons all shared. He would remind them about the rules with Post-it notes on their doors, instead of yelling at them like a prison guard. Teg had gotten a couple of those notes himself. One was for forgetting to make his bed, and the other was for leaving his clothes in the dryer too long. There weren't that many rules to follow, and Teg made a vow to try harder. The Post-it notes kind of cracked him up, though. So different than the prison environment he had come from.

During commercial breaks in the common room and over time, Teg heard Darnell's story. He had served a couple years, himself, for cocaine possession, and had once been a client at the same halfway house. A good and honest worker, Darnell had stayed clean and had gained the trust of state officials. So when the opportunity arose, he was given the job of house manager. Darnell loved his job. He took a special interest in each con, doing what he could to help them succeed. He encouraged the men to follow the same straight and narrow path he'd embraced for himself.

Darnell knew all about Teg's crime. He had the paperwork. But he didn't know much else. Teg wasn't much of a talker and kept his stuff bottled up inside. Regardless, a bond was beginning to form. Darnell's parents had given him a hundred dollar Macy's gift card for his birthday. There wasn't a thing he needed, though. So, he let Teg have the card to buy himself some new threads and drove him into the city for the shopping spree.

One night, Teg and Darnell were alone in the common room, watching a Braves Game on the 32" flat screen TV. The Braves were playing the Cincinnati Reds at Turner Field. They shared a bowl of pretzels and drank coke in real glasses with lots of ice. Both men despised the Reds, a feeling that was shared by almost all fans in the state of Georgia. The reason for the rivalry was long forgotten.

Teg had his feet up on a tattered ottoman. He'd had a long day at work and he reveled in the opportunity to relax and chill. Darnell was in a recliner nearby with his feet up as well. The two men were mostly quiet, watching the game. Of course, they hooted and hollered when Brian McCann hit a hard line drive. In the fifth inning, a home run by Chipper Jones had both men on their feet, yelling, and high-fiving.

During the seventh inning stretch, Darnell looked over at Teg.

"You think you'll move back home with your old man when your time here is done? I understand he don't live too far from here."

"Nope."

"You made any plans at all?"

"Nope."

"You got any other family you can stay with?"

"Nope."

"You can't stay here forever, man. You feeling me? In six months you'll be done here. You gotta start working on your future. Maybe take some classes at night. Get yourself a trade. Track down your mama or somebody you can move in with. Eventually, get your own place. You feeling me?"

Teg nodded, never taking his eyes off the screen. He wasn't about to share his story with Darnell. Not now . . . not ever.

Teg was raised by his daddy, Angus, over in Cabbage Town about five miles from the halfway house. The two of them lived alone. Teg's mama had run off when he was six, and Teg hadn't seen her since. Even worse, she'd left on Teg's birthday, and he would never forgive her for that.

Angus Duke was a nasty, mean drunk. He didn't work anymore like he did when Teg's mama was there. Angus started staying home, soon after she left, receiving disability checks for a back injury. He said he got it lifting boxes. His daddy had worked in a similar warehouse to the one that Teg worked at now. As soon as Angus got his check, he'd go straight to the liquor store. By the time Teg got home from school, his daddy would be staggering and angry. It wouldn't take much for the boy to irritate Angus and then the beatings would come . . . sometimes with a belt and sometimes with fists. There was no one there anymore to protect him.

One day when Teg was seven, he spilled a whole gallon of orange juice on the kitchen floor. He hadn't meant to. It had been sitting on the top shelf of the fridge and was almost full. It was too heavy for the little boy, and he shouldn't have tried to get it down by himself. But he was thirsty and his daddy was sitting on the couch with a bottle of gin watching a movie. He didn't want to bother him and get him riled up. So he thought he'd get the juice all by himself. The lid hadn't been properly closed when his father had opened it that morning to mix with his breakfast vodka. And he had pushed the jug all the way back in the fridge out of Teg's reach . . . almost. Teg used the tips of his fingers to scoot the gallon jug closer. The jug teetered when Teg had it halfway over the edge. He tried to catch it as it toppled forward, but it was too late. The orange juice crashed to the floor, caving in the plastic container, popping the lid, and sending the sticky liquid flying everywhere.

Angus heard the crash and came stumbling into the kitchen. "BOY! LOOK WHAT YOU'VE DONE!"

Teg cowered in the corner beside the fridge, making himself as small as he could. He knew what was coming. His daddy pulled off his belt. Teg covered his head, taking most of the blows on his arms and back.

He screamed. "NO DADDY. PLEASE, NO. I'M SORRY."

Angus jerked him up and over to the kitchen table. He unbuttoned the boy's pants and pulled them down to his ankles, underwear, too. He'd beat Teg before on his naked bottom and the child screamed in fear.

Angus picked Teg up by the back of his shirt and threw him down hard, face first on the table. This knocked the breath out of Teg, shocking him into silence. Angus finished pulling off the boy's pants and underwear and threw them across the room. He spread the child's legs.

"Your mama ran off cause of all your whining. A man's got needs. I ain't no homo. I just need me a tight hole."

Teg's screams were ignored by the residents of Cabbage Town. The folks in the neighborhood tended to mind their own business. They would hear those same screams for many years to come.

CHAPTER 12
MIXING, MISSING, AND MESSED UP

Saturday morning, while I baked Corn Puff Munchies, Streusel Coffee Cake, Chocolate Chip cookies, and crispy Ginger cookies with his mom, Dan carried the old microwave to the dump. I didn't bother telling it goodbye, but I did kiss Dan at the door.

Nancy asked me, right away, if I'd been to the salon. I told her "Nope. Just a Sharpie touch-up."

My mother-in-law commented, "Your hair looks lovely." I thought her fluffy white curls looked gorgeous as well and told her so.

Under Nancy's supervision, and Tom Smith's recipe, I stirred Karo syrup, butter, and brown sugar in a saucepan on the stovetop to pour over the corn puffs waiting over on the table in a disposable turkey roaster. I felt like a proper cook. I was even wearing an apron.

I love chatting with my mother-in-law and finding out the latest goings on at Heartwood Estates, an assisted living facility walking distance from our house. That day, she was full of stories and kept me entertained as we baked.

"We had a little excitement, yesterday."

"Oh? Do tell."

"Well . . . the police, fireman, and ambulance people were all here. They made us all come downstairs to the lobby."

"Oh, my! Why? What happened?"

"They lost a lady. Her name is Gladys."

"At Heartwood? How?"

"No one knew. They brought us downstairs and searched all of our apartments, the kitchen, and the cleaning closets. They couldn't find her anywhere."

I was intrigued.

"Then!" she said with great drama.

I was on the edge of my seat.

"The lady, Evelyn that lives in the apartment across from where they do the jigsaw puzzles told the police that her car keys were missing. Only five or six residents have cars. And she's one of them, however, she is missing a leg. It was amputated because of her diabetes, and so, she doesn't drive anymore. She gets other people to go get cigarettes for her, though, and they use her car. But, she hadn't given anyone permission yesterday."

"You think Gladys stole Evelyn's car?"

"Oh, I know she did. They put out an APB on the car and found her in Columbus two hours away. Gladys told them she was going to Florida."

I laughed. "So did they put her in the slammer?"

"No, but they did put an ankle monitor on her. She was sitting outside with a suitcase when you picked me up."

"That lady in the trench coat that was sitting in the rocker?"

"Yep. They better keep an eye on her. She's going to make a break for it. And, you and Dan, don't you dare leave your keys in your car."

I couldn't wait for my husband to hear this story. He was at the dump, though, longer than normal. On his return, Dan selected a cookie from the cooling rack and said, "You should see how they've upgraded the dump. It's really something."

"Perhaps I could arrange a field trip with a group of girlfriends, maybe the Widow's Club, or my pottery ladies, or the PenPal Writing Group. And, then, we could go out for drinks afterward. Want to join me and my friends for an evening at the dump, Nancy?" I removed the pan from the hot stove eye, stirred in a teaspoon of baking soda, and watched as the mixture began foaming.

My mother-in-law giggled. "Well, if there's going to be wine . . . sure."

Dan ignored our sarcasm and scooped up some corn puff munchies from the first batch. He doesn't mind my pottery class or my writing group. But, my membership in the Widow's Club makes him nervous. I guess it's because he's alive and well, and

41

the rest of the husbands are not. I think he worries that I'll do something to make myself legit. The ladies had waived the dead husband requirement for me, mainly because I'm married to a golfer.

He steered the conversation back to the dump. "They have these deep pits now. One is for furniture. One is for appliances. You just toss stuff in. It's pretty amazing . . . so are these things." He reached for more, but his mom smacked his hand with her wooden spoon.

"Wait until they've baked," she said.

I don't know why, but as I stirred the caramel sauce, it popped into my head to wonder if one of those pits at the dump held a little girl's tiny body.

I shivered.

Later, after we had stored all of the baked goods in proper tins, Dan was outside leaf blowing, and Nancy was resting in the living room, I went out to the porch and called my good friend and fellow artist, Alan Kuykendall.

He sounded tired. "Hi. What's up?"

Usually when I call Alan, I'm dragging him into some ridiculous . . . requiring hours of work . . . a project like a giant tree sculpture full of birdhouses, a fifty-foot train mural, or a fence made out of 150 eight foot colored pencils.

"You ever go down to the dump to forage for supplies?"

"No. It's against the law."

"Well, do you go down there when it's closed and no one is around to catch you?"

"Of course. Why?"

"Have you ever smelled a dead body down there?"

"Noooo. I can't say that I have. The place stinks of garbage, because . . . well, because it's a dump. Dead bodies have their own smell. I would notice. You on another case?"

"No, I'm not on a CASE. I'm not a detective. I was just wondering. So if you do go back and if you do smell something, will you call me?"

"Sure. I'll be glad to." Alan is used to me. This comes from twenty years of working together on absurd projects. He rarely questions me. I knew without a doubt, he'd probably go to the dump by the next day, just to see what it smelled like.

After I finished chatting with Alan, I went to the living room and turned on the TV to my DVR saved episode of Judge Judy. I kept the volume low, so I wouldn't wake Nancy snoozing on the couch. Roxie hopped up on the loveseat and lay down next to me. I watched the show while I absently stroked my cat's fur. She nuzzled my arm and purred with a deep growly rumble. And then, as she always does, she yawned and did a fake stretch of her paws. As she stretched, she unsheathed her claws and sank them deep into my upper thigh. I jumped up rubbing my leg and glared at her. "Why do you do that? Why?" No answer. Just another yawn. I sat back down . . . the petting over. Roxie snuggled closer and went to sleep with her head on my wounded leg. I do believe she is bi-polar.

Roxie has no idea how lucky she is to live in our home. Or if she does know, she doesn't care. It was in our wedding vows that I would never own a cat. This was not the wedding vows at the church. These were private vows Dan and I made over glasses of wine, one late night a few days before the wedding.

In addition to swearing I would never get a cat, I promised I wouldn't give my husband-to-be a hard time about golf, and I never have. In fact, I'm just as upset as he is when it rains on a Saturday and he can't play. I love my husband dearly, but I also love my house to myself. When he's home, he messes with my routine.

Dan's vows to me included not fussing when I make a mess in my wood shop. Sometimes that extends to the kitchen table, the screened porch, and the garage. He nicely turns a blind eye to the disarray of my various projects. And Dan vowed to not make fun of my cooking. I am sure there are times when he's struggled with that one, especially when Pam eggs him on.

We were both pretty good at honoring all of our vows . . . the traditional love and honor vows made at the Church, as well as our personal vows. What we didn't count on was having children. Our middle child, Leslie, brought several stray cats home over the years. I winced the first time. But, Leslie reminded us that she had made no such vow. Dan would have nothing to do with the cats, of course, but he wouldn't tell his beautiful child, no.

Roxie was the last of these feline intruders. She showed up at our front door fourteen years ago in the arms of one of Leslie's friends, begging us to give her a home. And so we did. Dan, who had always snarled at previous cats, actually chuckled at the tiny tabby kitten trying to jump over a blade of grass in the front yard. He gallantly fished her out of the pool when our pet rabbit pushed her in. It became very clear that a bond had formed, though Dan has always denied it.

Leslie is grown and gone now, a teacher in Washington DC. Her father never once suggested that she take Roxie with her. I rubbed my leg again and looked down at our kitty cat. Roxie looked so sweet and innocent sleeping next to me. I wondered for the hundredth time why she had such a mean streak. She had never suffered abuse. She could sleep wherever she wished. And her food and water bowls were always full and fresh. She had never scratched or bit Dan like she had me, on a daily basis. Again I asked, "What makes you so evil?" She purred in response. Yep. Bi-polar. I was fairly sure that explained it.

CHAPTER 13
THE FIRST RAIN
(Two Weeks Earlier)

Teg took his break outside where the smoker's hung out. He had never so much as tasted a cigarette nor a drop of hard liquor. He'd have a beer now and then, but that was all. And only if he had time enough to get the smell off of him before he went home. The halfway house had a zero tolerance for alcohol.

The only real rule Teg violated was the weapon policy. He had bought a cheap hunting knife from the Quickie Mart. They sold them right at the checkout counter. He kept it in his sock all day while he was at work. At home, he would plunge it in the ground in one of the shrubs before he went in the front door. Trimming the hedges at the halfway house was one of Teg's chores so it was unlikely to be found there by anyone else.

He looked at the clouds a good distance away and knew rain was coming later in the day. Teg hated it when Darnell picked him up, so around two o'clock, Teg lied to his boss, claiming a stomach ache, and began the walk home. When he got to the school, he stopped and looked in the fence. The rain was close and a few large drops splattered on the pavement. One of the teachers blew her whistle and started waving the children to come into the building.

Teg watched one pretty black haired girl of around nine or ten with long pigtails down her back. She carried a Harry Potter book in one hand and wore a short plaid dress, white socks, and black Mary Janes. A pudgy girl ran up giggling beside her, blocking his view. Irritated, Teg closed his eyes and imagined being on a date with the dark haired girl, taking apart those pigtails slowly, running his fingers through the wavy tresses. His right hand voluntarily made this motion, his fingers spread. His left hand moved down to an area it shouldn't. He went to a dark place, hardly aware.

Silence. When Teg opened his eyes the playground had cleared. He shrugged and turned back to the sidewalk and continued the walk home.

He was a half mile away when Darnell pulled up beside him. "Get in the car, Teg." There was tension in his voice.

Teg climbed into the passenger seat.

"Sorry. Were you coming to get me, man? I didn't know it was going to rain."

Darnell didn't respond. The tight grimace on his face told the ex-con that something was wrong.

They pulled in the driveway. It was still early and no one else was home. Darnell shut off the engine and leaned forward, resting his head on the steering wheel.

"Teg, man. I can't help you with this one and I can't write you up on a Post-it note either." Darnell closed his eyes. He was grieving a loss. He thought he'd made progress with this one.

"Is this cause I left early? I had a stomach ache. I told the boss and I...."

"Shut up! No. And you know that's not why. You stopped at that school and you jerked off in front of those little girls. The teacher called the cops on you. They called me within the minute and asked me to handle it. I can't save you from this. I'm calling your parole officer. You're sick. Sick! I'm sorry, man."

Teg reached over calmly and grasped a handful of Darnell's dreads. He jerked his hand back a few inches, then forward, and slammed Darnell's face hard into the steering wheel. Blood splattered from the broken nose. Before Darnell could scream, Teg pulled the knife from his sock and slit the man's throat. He sat with Darnell, his hand resting on the back of the neck, as the life drained out.

"I'm sorry, too, man."

CHAPTER 14
SIXTH SENSE, NO SENSE, OR NONSENSE?

Pam called just as I sat down at the table to eat my lunch. I was savoring the leftover lasagna, warmed up in my new Panasonic turbo, inverted convection microwave oven, now sitting snuggly under my spice cabinet. Roxie was asleep on top of the refrigerator, undisturbed by the sounds of ice falling from the ice maker below her.

"Whatcha doing?" Pam asked.

"Eatin unch," I responded with my mouth full of food. I swallowed. "What are you doing?"

"Well, I WAS eating lunch, myself . . . A bowl of Captain Crunch . . . Until you ruined it."

"What did I do?"

"My cereal tastes like garlic."

I looked at the crunchy garlic toast in my hand, reheated using the convection setting on my new fancy Panasonic Microwave that featured more buttons than the Hyatt Regency elevator.

"How do you do that?"

"It's called 'intuition.' I've told you that before . . . a hundred times."

"It's seriously creepy."

My twin has always been hyper tuned into me . . . my thoughts, my actions, my feelings. I don't understand it and I don't share the skill. I wasn't jealous that she could do this sixth sense thing. I wouldn't, in a million years, want to be saddled with that ability. Or if I do have it deep inside somewhere, I ignore it. Who knows? Maybe I just fight it off. Pam embraces everything . . . every weird thing on the planet.

"Are you coming down here, today?" I asked, laying my garlic toast on a saucer. Maybe in a few minutes, Pam could eat her cereal before Captain Crunch sunk to the bottom of the bowl in a milky orange slush.

"Have you looked outside? It's pouring rain, again. I'm not going anywhere. I'm going to stay in my recliner and watch some shows on the DVR. Right now I'm watching *The Apprentice*." Have you seen that show?"

"Nope. I can't stand Donald Trump with his orange skin and poofy fake hair."

"Well, I like the show a lot. There's this girl named Omarosa and she's awful. I just watch to see what she'll do next. Last week she faked a ceiling falling on her head. And I love Donald Trump. You would too if you watched it."

"Not happening."

"You're missing a good show. He's brilliant. You never know. Trump could be President one day."

I laughed. "Like that's ever gonna happen."

Pam, indignant now, "I'm intuitive about these things."

"Pffffff . . . Just goes to show your intuition has its limits."

"Speaking of intuition, I had a dream last night."

"Uh oh." Pam's dreams are something else. I always listen to them. I don't necessarily believe them, but I do listen.

"I dreamed about that little girl in Carrollton . . . the one who's dad talked to you. She's alive."

"Oh, Pam. She couldn't be. I've been reading all the newspaper articles online from the Times-Georgian and the Star. Even the Atlanta Constitution covered it. I've read them all. She drowned in the Little Tallapoosa. They found her little shirt a mile downstream."

"Why were you researching the case?"

"I thought she might be in the dump. Don't ask. But, she couldn't be. She drowned in the river."

"But they didn't find her. Right?"

"No, they didn't. But she's been gone for days. She's dead. Has to be."

"No she's not. If the rain stops, I'm coming down there tomorrow."

"You are welcome to come. FOR A VISIT. Nothing else. We are NOT detectives. Do you hear me?"

"I hear you."

"I'll make you something for lunch in my new fancy Microwave. Something better than cold cereal. I swear, I think this thing may have a conveyor belt that loads the dishwasher. I wouldn't doubt it. It's got all the bells and whistles and I . . . ."

I heard the distinct crunch of cereal and said my goodbyes. My sister is a nut.

I thought some more about Pam tasting garlic while she was eating her Captain Crunch. Who eats cereal for lunch? Just for meanness, I took another bite of my toast and chewed it slowly, savoring the garlic. The only sixth sense I have is that if I run into a cobweb I know there is probably a spider nearby. If I wake up with an aching right knee . . . which I did that very morning . . . I know it is going to rain. That's enough intuition for me.

CHAPTER 15
CARA'S JOURNAL AND SKETCH BOOK

Daddys sleeping. Im trying hard not to wake him up. Theres a squirl by the river eating a nut. Hes soooo cute. This is a picture of the squirl. I think hes trying to tell me something. This is his acorn. My Daddy told me he was proud of me today and that Im smart like my Mama. We are going to come back to this river after the rains come and see how the river looks when its all grown up.

CHAPTER 16
DEAR DEER

Dan came home early and went for a walk on the Greenbelt while I cooked dinner. Despite having a new microwave, I decided to give cooking on the stove another try. I had poured through various old cookbooks from a musky box in the attic, settling on Betty Crocker, because good old Betty used ingredients I actually had.

I preheated the oven and began slicing lemons and garlic. I sautéed the garlic in a skillet with sliced Vidalia onions and a little olive oil. My cookbook called these "aromatics" and, smelling them, I thought they were aptly named. I layered this in a casserole with the lemon slices. Then using paper towels, I patted down a butterflied chicken that the nice Publix butcher had prepared for me. I laid the chicken on top and drizzled the sides with a half cup of Pinot Grigio. I popped the dish into the oven and set the timer. When the smells began drifting through my house and the fire alarm stayed silent, I felt as accomplished as when I finished a painting. For side dishes, I heated some canned green beans and deli mashed potatoes in the microwave. Dan shouldn't expect me to become all Martha Stewart in one day.

The September weather was mild for a change and gently breezy, so we decided to dine on the porch.

"This is delicious." Dan was delighted with his dinner. "You really cooked this yourself? I'm impressed."

I vowed to try some other recipes soon. He took another bite and glanced over at my easel.

"I thought you were painting mountains. Who is that?"

"No idea. Believe it or not, it's the same painting turned sideways. By the way, you can eat the lemons."

"Really?"

Dan turned back to his plate and tasted a lemon. "Yum." Then he tilted his head and looked again at the painting.

"Interesting. I like it. Not as much as this dinner, but I like it. She looks girlish and womanly at the same time. Who is she?"

I smiled. "I have no idea. How was your walk?"

"This weather is great. Lots of folks out on the Greenbelt. I saw a mother deer and two babies down at the trail head."

"Nice. Lizzie and I saw them on our street the other day."

"Funny how you never see a buck with them."

"No, City Boy. That's normal. Remember Bambi? The buck leaves after they mate and the mom raises them on her own. The buck goes off and does his own thing."

"Hmmm. Seems like they've got that right. Why can't people do it that way? The dad could have all the fun and then leave and let the mom do all the raising."

"You men already do that. It's called golf."

Dan chuckled and clicked my glass of wine with his. A lovely evening . . . It would be a while before we would dine alone again.

CHAPTER 17
RUNNING MAN

For a brief moment, Teg considered taking Darnell's car, body, blood, and all. Soon, the other residents would return to the halfway house. It wouldn't be long before the police would begin searching. The last thing he needed to do was to be driving his car. They would know it was him soon enough. He didn't need to make it easy for them.

So, instead, he moved Darnell over to the passenger seat, removing the floor mat before he did so. He carried the mat around to the driver's side and placed it over the blood. Starting the ignition, Teg drove the car around the side of the house and parked it in the back directly under the window.

The routine of every ex-con who lived at the house was to enter through the front door and either plop down in the common room or go upstairs to their assigned bedroom and rest until dinner time. Stuart, thankfully, was on duty to cook that night and the kitchen window looked over the backyard. If it was anyone else, this could be a problem. But parking the car close to the wall directly underneath the window ledge might work, especially since Stuart wore bottle thick eye glasses. There were no hedges there, and Teg was pretty sure that Stuart's blurry view would be over the car to the yard beyond. This should work unless Stuart stood on his tiptoes, leaned over the sink, and then down. Even then, his visibility would be poor and besides, what possible reason would he have to do that? None, that Teg could imagine. This might work.

Car moved, Teg ran into the house and up the stairs to his room. He packed his duffle bag with a few clothes, stuffing the cash from his paychecks into a side pocket. The clock on the nightstand let him know he had about thirty minutes left if he wanted to be gone before the residents returned. He took a quick shower, taking the knife with him to make sure all of the blood was gone. He dressed in jeans and a grey hooded sweatshirt and returned the knife to the strap on his sock. Using his towel to pick them up, Teg stuffed his bloody garments between the mattress and box spring of his bed. He tossed the towel in with them.

He was ready to go, thrilled with the excitement of a life on the run. Teg walked halfway up the driveway, but a thought occurred to him and he turned and ran around the house to the backyard. He needed all the money he could get, so he opened the passenger door. Careful to avoid blood, he reached into Darnell's pocket and found his wallet. It had fourteen dollars in it. "I guess house managers don't make much," he thought. Teg shrugged and began his journey on foot.

The rain had stopped, at least for the moment. Teg had nowhere safe to go really, but he needed wheels and he knew where to get them. He hiked down back roads until he reached Cabbage Town and up the alley to the back side of his father's house. Peering in the dirty living room window through the plantation shutters, he could see Angus asleep in a tattered recliner. He barely recognized the shrunken old man. It had been twenty years since they had seen one another. Should he break in or just knock on the door?

Walking around to the front, Teg was surprised. "Nice Wheels." A black Ford Escape SUV sat in the driveway. It was a tank of a car. No way was his father the owner of this car. Teg returned to the window out back to wait, to watch.

A few minutes later, a woman came from the kitchen and into the living room with a glass of water. She held the glass tenderly to Angus's lips, helping him drink. She held a napkin under his chin to catch the dribble. And then, she knelt on her knees beside him, smiling and talking to him. The old man smiled back and nodded. The woman stood and patted his back and returned to the kitchen.

Teg was shocked. The woman was black. This was his daddy! And his daddy hated black people, always had. Teg just couldn't believe what he was seeing. The betrayal of it all . . . of his childhood . . . a great rage growing.

Teg heard the back door open. He turned and froze. The woman didn't see him. She walked out of the door with a garbage bag in her hand humming "*His Eye is on the Sparrow.*" She carried the bag to the outside can with her back to Teg. He pulled the sweatshirt over his head and leaned over to set it on the ground. Still bent at the waist, and watching, he withdrew the knife.

Now singing, the woman removed the lid and lowered the bag.

"*I sing because I'm happy, I sing because I'm free, For His eye is on the sparrow, and I know He watches me.*"

Teg crept closer. She spotted a piece of paper, a soiled napkin on the ground and stooped to pick it up and put it in the garbage can. That done, she replaced the lid, still singing the spiritual.

"*Let not your heart be troubled, His tender word I hear, And resting on His goodness, I lose my doubts and fears;*"

Teg shoved the blade between her shoulder blades. Twisting . . . turning . . . interrupting. The music stopped.

Teg dragged her into the kitchen and laid her on the floor. He cleaned up in the kitchen sink and then returned outside for his sweatshirt. He didn't put it on right away. He wasn't done. Instead, he hung the shirt from a chair, underneath the ceiling fan, the air blowing the garment like a victory flag.

Teg saw a purse on the kitchen table and rifled through it. He found some more cash, nearly a hundred dollars. That, plus Darnell's money and his own savings, came to almost four hundred. Some papers in the side pocket let him know she was some kind of a nurse. That made sense. His daddy probably had no say in who cared for him. He'd looked old and withered when Teg saw him through the slats of the blinds.

Teg also found an ID. The woman's name was Voncille White. "White!" Teg snorted. At the bottom of the purse, he found some mints and stuck them in his pocket. And he found a phone. Teg knew about cell phones. He'd seen the guards use them and Darnell had one, as did the dudes he worked with at the warehouse. He put that in his pocket, too. If he'd known that cell phones could be traced he'd probably have let it be, but there was a lot about the outside world he still didn't know yet.

Unfortunately . . . or fortunately for Teg . . . this phone couldn't be traced. Voncille had taken it from her fifteen-year-old son, Tyrone, earlier that morning. She knew a burner phone when she saw one. And she knew she hadn't bought it. Long suspecting her son was doing some drug dealing, she made him empty his pockets. She found the cash and took it, too and then smacked Tyrone across the side of his head. No son of hers was going to end up killed or in prison from running with the gangs. She'd be having a long talk with Tyrone when she got home from her shift. But he needed to get to school and she needed to get over to Mr. Duke's.

The lamp was on next to Angus and Teg could see much clearer. His daddy's right lip drooped from a stroke and his skin was a ghastly yellow color. Angus's emaciated body had shrunken to half the size he once was in his prime . . . in his meanest days.

"I reckon all that liquor's done pickled your liver, Daddy. You done turned yellow since I seen you." Teg said this as he walked into the room and around the chair so his father could see him square on. "Do you know who I am? It's been a long, long time."

"Ayaa," was all Angus could manage. Drool leaked from the side of his mouth. The room stunk of urine and Pinesol.

Teg wiped his daddy's drool with a cloth diaper that hung over the back of the green recliner.

"You able to talk old man?"

"Nyaaa Gaaaa."

"I guess not. That's too bad. I thought we could have us a conversation."

"Ya Tugg."

"That's right! Good job. It's Teg. I've come for a visit and of course to kill you."

Angus looked hard at him. His own eyes pleading. "Daaya at."

Teg knelt next to his father in the same spot and in the same way he'd seen the nurse do earlier. "What's that? Want me to put you out of your sorry misery, old man?"

Teg held his knife up. Now clean, he wiped it back and forth on his daddy's pant leg, like this would sharpen the blade. Angus watched this and then looked back into the eyes of his son. He was afraid and Teg could see it. This made Teg smile.

Teg continued, "I should kill you. You sure deserve it. All them years of beatin's . . . and other things. Yep, nobody could blame me for taking you out old man. And look around. Who'd miss you?"

Obeying the command, Angus darted his eyes around the room. He wondered where his nurse had got off to.

Teg laughed, "You sit in your own piss . . . Or shit in your own piss." He laughed again. "Both I guess. Thing is, it's kind of nice to watch you suffer some." He turned the knife and jabbed the handle of it hard into his father's abdomen where he thought the cirrhosis infected liver might be.

"Aughhh," Angus yelped.

"Yeah man. I think I'm gonna let you live. Let you suffer. Let you die a long and painful death before you go off to Hell."

"Argah . . . tag."

He stood up. Teg tossed the knife in the air, letting it spin. He caught it by the handle in his right hand. "Then again . . ."

He sliced his daddy's throat. But not deeply like he had Darnell's. Teg cut just enough that it would take a while for Angus to bleed out. Then he walked across the room and sat on the sofa to watch his daddy die. It took a long, long time.

As the clock on the wall ticked off the minutes, Teg watched the very moment his father's misery ended. It was a fascinating thing to observe up close. Death occurred with a peculiar color change, that happened with a horizontal line ascending up Angus's neck until it disappeared out the top of his head . . . changing the skin from yellow to grey, and the eyes from black and penetrating to dull glass. And with that, it was over.

Teg returned to the kitchen, stepping over Voncille. For the third time that day, he washed the knife and returned it to his sock. He washed the blood from his hands and arms and pulled his hoodie back over his head. Then he found a narrow cabinet full of empty grocery store bags and began stuffing them with all the food he could find.

Teg picked up Voncille's keys next to her now empty purse and carried the grocery bags to the back of the SUV. He drove through Atlanta slowly. It was after six, but traffic was still heavy. Teg was frightened by the number of vehicles that surrounded him, so he didn't mind driving slow. He wouldn't risk speeding with no license anyway. The one way streets were a nightmare to navigate. Peachtree Road, Peachtree Street, Peachtree SW . . . the roads made no sense at all.

Making turns randomly, Teg found his way onto Spring Street. He had no idea where he was going and stayed in the right lane. The directions tucked away in his shirt pocket would be useful later. He just needed to go west. The road led him to Interstate 20 and he, first stopped, then merged onto the freeway with impatient drivers behind him honking for him to go. I-20 west wasn't as bad as downtown and he finally relaxed and settled into the drive. He turned on the radio, changing the dial from gospel to a country station, and sang along to Lady Antebellum, as he drove west with a purpose . . . a possible destination . . . and perhaps a plan.

Tell me have you ever wanted
Someone so much it hurts?
Your lips keep trying to speak
But you just can't find the words . . .

CHAPTER 18
NO BODY, NO WILLY

Dan helped me get my groceries out of the back of the Trailblazer and carried them into the kitchen.

"Alan Kuykendall called while you were gone."

"Hmmm. Wonder why he didn't call my cell. What did he say?"

"He said to tell you that there didn't seem to be any dead body smells at the dump. What the heck are you up to now? And does this have anything to do with why your sister is on her way here?"

"No. It's an art thing."

"Oh."

Dan didn't question that and I knew he wouldn't. He would be afraid I would start going into detail on some contemporary art project that would glaze his eyes over . . . about like mine do when he talks about regression analysis, attestation of compliance, and chart vectors. Some parts of our work are best left separate.

I chopped the chicken off of the rotisserie bird I'd bought at Ingles and put the pieces into a bowl. Dan diced some celery as I stirred in the mayo.

"Did you feed Roxie while I was at the store? I didn't see her this morning."

"I did. It ate its cat food and then came back in the house. It's asleep on the World Book Encyclopedias in the living room." He dumped the celery into my bowl.

I stirred in mayo, walnut bits, and dried cherries. "Why do you call our cat an IT? She's a SHE."

Dan split the croissants and put them on a plate. "How do you know it's a she? I've never seen a birth certificate."

I finished mixing the chicken salad. "There's no willy."

Dan sliced the rind off of the cantaloupe. "Willy? Did you call it a willy?"

I rinsed my stirring spoon and replaced it with an identical serving spoon. I have no idea why. "SHE is fourteen years old.

SHE has been spayed . . . not neutered . . . SHE does not have a willy. The evidence is pretty straightforward."

Dan spooned some chicken salad onto a croissant with the clean serving spoon and put it on his plate. "I'll think about not saying IT if you will stop saying WILLY."

I cut the cantaloupe into smaller bite sized pieces. "That's what Eleanor Hoomes calls it."

"IT? I thought we weren't using IT." Dan popped a piece of cantaloupe into his mouth and a handful next to his sandwich.

I handed Dan a napkin. "Eleanor Hoome's . . . You know her from my PenPal Writer's group . . . Anyway, Eleanor's granddaughter, Victoria, has a cute little ankle biter Yorkie dog that had been playing outside. The dog's name is Toast. Isn't that adorable? Anyway, Toast got covered in leaves and sticks and Eleanor was trying to get them off his belly, but one of the sticks was stuck. She tried and tried to get it off. She finally asked Victoria to help. Victoria looked at what Eleanor was pulling on and said, 'That's not a stick Gran. That's his little willy.' Isn't that hilarious?"

"If you are trying to tell me to go pull on Roxie's willy, you can forget it." Dan opened a bag of ruffled potato chips.

I spooned green onion dip onto his plate next to the chips. One of the chips was folded the way I like them so I popped it into my mouth. After I crunched it up and swallowed I continued the conversation. "No. That's the point. Roxie doesn't HAVE a willy because Roxie is a girl. Go look."

"I have no intention of looking that close at IT." With that, my husband kissed my cheek and headed to the living room to watch the golf channel and eat his lunch.

Our whole marriage, this is how we fight.

CHAPTER 19
VACATION SPOT

Teg got off in Villa Rica for gas, a little pissed that Voncille hadn't had the common decency to fill her car up. It had been twenty years since he had put gas in a car and he wasn't quite sure how to do it. Teg went into the convenience store and, avoiding eye contact with the clerk, he threw a twenty on the counter. Back at the pump, Teg read the directions which confused him. Finally, watching a man at another pump, he figured it out. He was shocked, though, when he got in the car and realized that $20 barely gave him half a tank.

"You've gotta be shittin me." He'd been in prison a long time.

Teg decided to stay off the freeway, take the back roads and find a place to hole up. He turned onto Highway 166 and found himself in the little unincorporated town of Fairplay. A little way down, he passed a seedy motel and did a U-Turn. Across the street from the Baymont Inn was a gas station. It looked closed and in need of remodeling. Plywood covered the windows. Perfect!

He pulled the car behind the store and got out. In the dark, he looked across the street and studied the motel. The room closest to the office had a car in front of the door. The next room nothing, then another car at the third door. He remembered this pattern, taught to him by another con. Motels would rent every other room when census was down and then fill in between if census was up. So, it was safe to bet, no one would be in the last room. He reclined his seat and slept in the SUV until the sun came up.

The next morning, he got out of the car and peed in the grass. Peering around the building, he could see a young maid pushing a cart outside the door at Room 3. He waited until she went in the room before he crossed the street.

Alice poured cleanser into the toilet, sprayed down the shower, and began stripping the bed. She carried the sheets out the door to load onto her cart and swap out with fresh ones. She jumped, startled as a man was standing next to her cart.

Regaining composure, Alice smiled. "Good morning, sir."

"Morning, young lady."

"You a guest here? Do you need something?" Alice was protective of her shampoos and coffee packets.

"Actually, I was a guest here a week ago. I think I left an important paper in my room. Think you could let me look?"

"Sir, we would have cleaned the room thoroughly after you left."

"I'm sure you would have, pretty lady. But I'd laid it flat on the shelf in the closet, so I'm hoping you might have missed it."

Alice blushed. No one ever called her pretty. And the man was right. Something like a flat piece of paper could easily be overlooked on that high shelf.

"Which room?"

"120."

Alice was surprised. She couldn't remember the last time they had someone all the way to the end room. But she didn't work every day, so it was possible.

She pulled out her jangle of keys and Teg followed her to Room 120.

Alice waited outside while Teg searched. She didn't watch him, and so, she didn't notice that he went into the bathroom and unlatched the window. He pulled a piece of paper from his pocket he had found in Voncille's glove box. He came out waving the paper in his hand. Alice closed the door and made sure it was locked.

"Thanks . . . What's your name pretty girl?"

"Alice." She blushed again. At eighteen, she wasn't used to very much attention and lately, she was getting a lot. The pool boy had been flirting with her, and that was enough to make her giddy and lay awake all night thinking of him. But this man was older. There was something weird about his eyes. They were dark and soulless. A chill ran through her. Suddenly uncomfortable, she stepped off the walkway into the grass. A little distance made her feel safer.

"You have a good day, sir." Alice walked briskly back to her cart.

When the girl disappeared into Room 103, Teg slipped back across the street to the SUV. He waited until dark to return to the motel, creeping quietly in the shadows. The unlatched window slid open easily and Teg slithered through and into the room.

Teg kept the lights off and the curtains closed. The TV wouldn't put out much light especially when he turned it on the swivel shelf so that the back faced the window, so he was able to watch NBC to see if his face was in the news. The glow of the screen gave him enough light to see around the room. He kept the volume low. Nothing, yet, but it was a matter of time before he would be exposed in the news.

Teg set the alarm for 5:00 a.m. so he could be out before the maids came through. They probably wouldn't clean his room. No reason to, but he'd leave just to be sure. A shower, a so-so dinner from a loaf of bread and pimento cheese from Angus's house . . . best to use up the perishables first . . . and Teg was ready for bed. It had been a busy day. He chose the bed furthest from the door and crawled under the covers, wearing just his shorts. He watched TV until he drifted off. He slept well, his knife under his pillow.

The next morning, Teg left the motel before the sun was up. He had carefully made the bed and took his garbage with him. He even refolded his now dry towel so that no one would know it had been used. He walked back to the car and napped in the driver's seat as the sun rose. At eleven . . . checkout time . . . he walked to the side of the store and watched the homely Alice push her cart into Room 101. When she finished in 105, she was done. She didn't open any other door. Nice. He could stay in Room 120 as long as he wished. Teg took a long walk in the woods behind the motel. He slipped back in his room, with more food from the SUV, when the coast was clear.

CHAPTER 20
JAM

Pam arrived around noon and handed me a jar. The label said, "PAM JAM – PEACH." Dan had already eaten his lunch, and he was out puttering around in the front yard with a rolling thing that makes holes in the ground. I've never understood the purpose for that, as the moles made plenty of holes. Roxie was too old now to hunt them down. Dan says it's for aeration. Whatever . . .

"Yum. I love your jams." I placed the jar in the fridge beside the already open PAM JAM – VERY BERRY she had given me a few weeks before. "Congrats on getting peaches again this year."

"Deer didn't get a one of them."

Pam had gone to elaborate methods to protect her peaches from deer, including a singing Christmas tree, sonar radiating devices, aluminum foil, a fake owl, and a nasty looking urine soaked stuffed dog hanging from the branches. We were just past her second summer of successful peach picking.

I poured my sister a glass of iced tea, and we sat down at the kitchen table to eat.

Pam took a bite of her chicken salad sandwich. "Mmm, this is good."

"Thanks. I love this recipe."

"Dan must be thrilled that you've learned to make something that doesn't gag him."

"Dan loves my cooking. He chopped some of the ingredients for me."

"What are these dark bits in here? Flies?"

"No. Dried cherries."

She took another bite. "This is delicious. I'm going to ask you something I've never asked before."

"What's that?"

"Can I have the recipe?"

I laughed. "It's Lizzie's chicken salad recipe. But, sure. I'll write it down for you, before you leave this afternoon."

"Actually, I was hoping to stay a few days. I have a suitcase in the car."

I was surprised. We hadn't discussed this at all. "Something wrong?"

"No. I've decided to make that fairy garden you suggested when we were in Athens. I started with the ceramic fairy house you made me that I found in your purse. Remember?"

I nodded. "I remember you made fun of it. But, I'm glad. You need a hobby now that your peach war with the deer is over, and you've completed the task of nearly getting your sister killed."

Pam's husband Sam had disappeared years ago under mysterious circumstances that we no longer talked about, and like mine, her children were grown and gone. I worried about her being lonely. Retired from teaching, Pam thrived on having projects to keep her busy.

"I was thinking I could go to your pottery class with you . . . make some myself."

"The girls at the Blue Heron would love having you. We can go tonight. Finish eating and help me change the sheets in the guest room."

After we readied the guest room, we took some of Pam's jam over to Nancy's apartment at Heartwood. A year before, I had given Nancy three little pop-top glass jars, and I kept them filled with a variety of jams and preserves. She loved taking them into the dining hall, pooh poohing the packaged jellies that came with her toast.

As she and Pam chatted, I looked through her cabinets and refrigerator for the jars. I could only find two.

"Nancy. Are you missing a jar?"

She looked embarrassed. "I had a little accident last week. I dropped one of them on the floor."

"Oh. Did it break?" I hated the idea of her trying to clean up broken glass and sticky jam.

"It did. But, I didn't know it. I picked it up and took it to breakfast with me. This lady, Martha, from the first floor, was eyeing it so I offered her some. I had a waffle and didn't use it for myself. When I got back to my room and went to put it in the fridge, I noticed a sliver of glass was missing."

"A sliver?"

"Well, it was a chunk really. About an inch long."

Pam looked horrified. "I hope that lady didn't eat the glass."

Nancy said, "Me, too. I looked everywhere for the missing piece, though. And I couldn't find it."

"Has she, ummm, has Martha had any problems?" I asked.

Nancy leaned forward. "Well, we had two women die this week, and I held my breath until I made sure it wasn't Martha."

I know it was macabre, but both Pam and I laughed.

I said, "That's good, I guess."

Nancy whispered, "But, I did hear her blood pressure was low."

CHAPTER 21
ROOM MATES

Teg had been in the motel off and on for nearly a week. He was getting cabin fever. Might as well be back in prison with all the freedom he had. A couple of times, he was tempted to stroll into the lobby of the motel office and enjoy the free hot breakfast they served. But of course, he couldn't do that.

He would still leave every morning to take long walks in the woods and get supplies from the car out back of the old store. And he'd stay in the shadows now and then and watch the comings and goings from the motel. One day, there were five cars parked out front, all the way to Room 109, and he got a little nervous. But that was all and he was okay.

Every other day, a pool boy would come and skim leaves from the greenish waters of the pool that no one in their right mind would ever swim in. The skinny pool boy's face was covered in acne, the kind that forever leaves deep scars.

Teg watched the pool boy roll up the pump hose as the homely cleaning girl, Alice, came out of Room 105 with her cart. He watched how their eyes met. Something going on between those two. He'd thought so for days.

Shit, he was bored. He'd stooped this low, watching an ugly boy and an ugly girl flirt with each other like it was his own private soap opera . . . his only entertainment. Enough was enough. But, now wasn't the time to run. His picture was finally all over the news. One of the halfway house residents had walked around back to have a smoke and found the car and Darnell. Apparently, no one had reported him missing the day before. Why would they? But they knew now.

Teg was the only resident unaccounted for so he was pinned for the crime immediately. Plus, the cops had gotten the initial call from the teacher and had contacted Darnell. So, it wasn't a big leap for them to know who to look for. Cops tossed his room and found the bloody clothes. They had the address to his father's house from

Darnell's files and found the bodies there as well. Somebody from something called Hospice was on the air earlier talking about the dead nurse. Teg didn't even know what a Hospice was . . . sounded like a fancy name for hospital. The story was being told on the national news channels, too.

Teg was big news, but he was also, stuck. He still had a lot of food in the SUV though. Enough for another week if he was careful. The news had not reported a description of the vehicle which Teg found odd. He knew the police had to know that he had stolen Voncille's car. It must be one of those evidentiary items they were keeping close to the vest. He couldn't imagine why. Tempted to go right then, he pulled the directions he had tucked into the console and studied them. It was just too early to leave the safety of the motel room and his daytime hideout behind the old store so he refolded the paper and put it in his pocket. He would have to be patient.

Now, even more on guard for police, Teg waited until dark to go back to his room. The nightly news had a big story about him. Everyone in the country could see his mug shot and hear what he'd done. That Alice girl. She'd seen him up close. How long before she recognized the man she'd let into Room 120? He couldn't stay there much longer. He'd seen enough on the television and clicked it off with the remote. Rolling onto his side so he faced the door, Teg drifted off to sleep.

Teg came awake suddenly . . . on guard . . . hand under his pillow on the knife handle. Someone was outside jiggling the knob. The door opened and he could see the silhouettes of two figures. He lay still in the bed. Whoever it was didn't turn the lights on. He heard giggling and then the sound of mattress springs as the couple fell on the other bed.

Alice and the pool boy, like Teg, they assumed the last room was safe to break into. And here they were sexing it up right next to him in the dark, unaware that he was there. He waited listening to their murmurings.

Teg heard clothing drop to the floor, passionate sounds, kissing. Like a porno one heard but couldn't see. The sounds of screwing, the slapping of flesh on flesh became louder, more intense. Teg felt his erection, and he slid his shorts down and off his legs.

Naked, now, Teg quietly slithered off the side of the bed and crawled on all fours across the carpet, knife in his right hand. He stood slowly beside the bed and grabbed the one on top by the hair. Short hair, so he knew it was the boy. Good. In the dark, he slit the boy's throat deep, severing the vocal cords, and laid him over beside the girl.

Alice was moaning with eyes closed and thought Joey was just changing positions. The scent of him was different and there was wetness on her shoulder. With the first thrust between her legs, she opened her eyes, realizing with horror that someone else was on top of her. The man clasped his hand over her mouth pushing hard on her face, and when he was done . . . when he was spent, he sliced her throat, too.

Obviously, Teg would have to leave now.

CHAPTER 22
THE BLUE HERON

Pam and I arrived at the Blue Heron around six. I carried in a set of small plates that I had been trimming at home and checked the shelf to see what had arrived from the bisque fire. I had a couple of platters and several tree pieces I had made for wall hangings. I would take those home to mount on old wood strips.

We walked past the wheel room, saying hi to Sweet Emily and Kyra who were busy throwing bowls and then into the main studio work room where I introduced Pam to Melanie Drew, the teacher, and then to the rest of my fellow students, Sweet Emily, Honey, Lois, Melissa, Kyra, and Sherry. Lizzie was there, too, but Pam's known her for years. Everyone was delighted to finally meet my twin. They'd heard lots of stories about her. Honey grabbed my sister up in a big bear hug.

Melanie rolled out a slab of recycled multicolored clay for Pam and showed her how to smooth it over a platter form. Lizzie took over from there while our teacher went to the kitchen to prepare our dinner.

Pam learned how to apply black underglaze to the clay, and was amazed at how fast it dried. Then Lizzie gave her some carving tools and a selection of designs. Pam chose a butterfly pattern and was soon lost in the activity of carving into the black glaze.

Melanie popped back in to explain Sgraffito to Pam. "It's an Italian word. Sgraffito describes the art of incising through a layer or layers of slip to expose the clay beneath, just as you are doing."

All around the tables was boisterous conversation and laughter. Some of it was a bit risqué, but we were all ladies of various ages and experiences and there were no rules other than to have fun.

"This got way too dry. I may need to use some oil."

"That's what he said." Melissa just couldn't resist.

"Try rolling it between your hands until the ridges soften."

"That's what she said."

Pam cracked up. "You girls are a hoot."

The occasional ding from Lizzie's phone meant another message from some guy on match.com was coming in and we'd quiet down and sip our wine and mold clay and wait patiently for her to read it to us.

"Oh my word. Listen to this one. '*You are so adorable. I hope you like ferrets.*' What kind of message is that to send the first time you contact a woman?"

"He surely lives in his parent's basement. Better skip him, Lizzie."

"Yep. He's a goner." She hit a button on her phone, forever canceling ferret guy.

Pam said, "No! That could be our brother. He has ferrets."

Laughter erupted from every workspace.

"Brett doesn't live in Mom's basement. So it isn't him."

Dulcie showed up late with a hot pan of buttered cornbread to go with Melanie's soup. The aroma was heavenly and filled the room.

Lizzie had taken upon herself months before, the task of teaching Sweet Emily about Southern ways. Sweet Emily . . . we all called her that . . . was a sociology professor at the university, but she looked like a teenager. She was from Ohio. She often traveled to Nepal to work on research for a religion project. She was a gentle soul and we all loved her.

Emily came in from the wheel room to show Pam a set of mugs from the finishing shelf that had been carved with the same Sgraffito process my sister was learning.

Lizzie asked her, "Hey Emily. Do you know the difference between Southern cornbread and Northern cornbread?"

We all perked up to see if Emily knew that Yankees put sugar in their cornbread, a ghastly sin to all of us.

"What?" Emily asked.

Melanie spoke slowly like Sweet Emily was a toddler. "Do . . . you . . . know . . . the difference between . . . Northern and Southern . . . cornbread recipes?"

She pondered the question before asking, "Does Yankee cornbread have the blood of Confederate soldiers in it?"

We howled. Honey yelled, "Score one for Sweet Emily!"

Pam examined the mugs.

"Wow. I love the little paisleys you've carved on those."

Sweet Emily said, "They're actually doodles. I doodle a lot at work and then bring the designs here. They look a lot better on clay than they do on paper."

Inspired now, I could see Pam's butterfly begin to emerge with intricate swirls on the wings. Honey showed her a few cool tricks with some textured rolling pins.

At eight o'clock, Melanie called us into the dining room. She had, as usual, set a lovely table with flowers in the center and hand-made plates and bowls at each unmatched chair. Dinner was almost always a soup and tonight was no exception. We all enjoyed a delicious tomato cabbage masterpiece with a loaf of fresh focaccia bread Melanie had bought at the Corner Café. And of course, we also had Dulcie's cornbread. We grated fresh parmesan from the Saturday Farmer's Market over our soup and a second bottle of wine was passed around. No one hurried and everyone joined in on the spirited chatter.

Melanie said, "Pam, we are so delighted you could join us."

"Thanks for having me. Now that I've finished my butterfly platter, can I make something else?"

"Absolutely. Do you have something in mind?"

"I want to make a fairy house with the bottom out of it so I can add lights. I'm going to build a fairy garden in my front yard."

This led to all kinds of fairy house ideas and we were all soon back in the studio workroom. Everyone put aside other projects to make a fairy house version of their own. Melissa and Lizzie's were very elaborate. Mine and Pam's looked like something the Flintstones would live in. Emily, Dulcie, and Sherry went outside and found leaves to use as a rooftop pattern. Lois and Kyra began making accessories like little park benches, fairy figurines, and mini mushrooms. Melanie finished in the kitchen and joined us, her little dog Molly in her lap. We all rethought our own designs as we watched Melanie make a gorgeous round fairy house with a tiny front porch and a chimney on the leaf-shaped roof. Lizzie had mastered the art of mini hinge making so I passed mine to her to help with my little open door.

The room got quiet with creative thought until Pam spoke up. "Tinkerbell could live in this little house."

Melanie said, "She sure could."

Pam picked up the house, looking through the little window. "I heard that little girl that disappeared on the Tallapoosa River loved Tinkerbell. I read that somewhere."

Lois said, "Yes. I did, too. Her dad was talking on TV in an interview. He was showing her Tinkerbell pajamas, and talking about how much she loved them. It was pitiful."

Kyra added, "I think so too. Do you all think she really drowned?" Her eyes were tear filled.

Kyra was a young stay-at-home mom to a house full of small children. I was not surprised that she would be sensitive to the missing Cara.

"That's what the cops say," responded Sherry. "They are pretty sure of it. I think the dad doesn't want to accept it."

Lois, the skeptic, said, "I always think it's the parent that did it."

Lizzie handed my newly hinged door fairy house back, and I chiseled out a four leaf clover on the tiny door. I didn't join the conversation. I knew Pam had a motive for bringing it up and I declined to participate. I saw Pam look my way, and knew she was about to drag me in when Lizzie's phone thankfully pinged.

"Ha Ha Ha. Girls listen to this . . . *'You look like wife material but I can only see you from the waist up. Do you have sturdy thighs? Let's meet at the Huddle House in Franklin to see what we have in common.'* . . . Delete and block Weirdo Number Two."

"Lizzie, how long are you going to keep doing this?" I laughed, grateful for the distraction.

"It's fun. I've refused to go out with any of them so far. But, I've been a widow for a year now and I get lonely. You never know when I might find another Prince Charming. I talked Deborah into signing up yesterday."

Deborah is a Widow's Club member, not a potter, but most of the girls know her.

Sherry rolled her eyes. "Oh my goodness. Deborah is on match.com? I can't wait to hear how that goes."

Pam was not going to let the missing child conversation drift away. "Did you know that little girl's daddy confronted Penny at Walmart? He wants her to help find his child."

I could have kicked her right then and there. Instead, I reached over and squooshed her fairy house. I knew it was childish, but I couldn't help myself. Pam responded by squooshing mine right back.

"Well, that backfired on you. I was making my fairy house for you."

"I don't care. You shouldn't have squooshed mine first."

"Girls, girls!" Poor Melanie wasn't used to having quarreling adult twins in her studio.

"I'm sorry," I said. "I didn't want Pam to bring that up."

Lizzie was adamant. "You have to tell us what happened."

"I don't guess you all want to hear about my microwave dying and buying a new one. It was quite the ordeal."

"NO." They all yelled at the same time.

I sighed and told them the whole story about meeting Leman Garrett. I left out the part about the pillowcases as I doubted they would care. However, I did tell them about the jerk that spit on my foot. They certainly didn't care about my microwave.

Melanie asked, "What reason does he have for thinking she didn't drown?"

"I have no idea."

"Well, we NEED to know," Kyra said.

"No, we don't. Why do WE need to know anything about this?"

"Look, Penny," Pam said. "Listen to your friends. You live in this community. You have to care. She's a little girl. What if it was one of yours?"

Pam knows right where to punch me in the stomach. Too bad, I couldn't punch her right back.

CHAPTER 23
THE PICNIC

Teg took to the back roads, avoiding cops and people. He spotted a discarded baseball hat on the side of the road and stopped to pick it up. A disguise, he could pull over his brow when he went in gas stations to pay for gas. His picture was surely seen by everyone by now. He had learned how much money he needed for a full tank so he wouldn't have to stop much. With no credit card, he would have no choice but to go inside to pay. His money was starting to dwindle. And he was sick and tired of driving aimlessly.

Teg wound his way past the University of West Georgia in Carrollton, up Highway 27 towards Bremen. He had to relieve himself bad, and so he found a parking space in a wooded area near a boat ramp and pulled over. No cars in sight there. As usual, he liked to do his business in the woods and so he started walking. He walked a good three-quarters of a mile, spotting another boat ramp along the river and couldn't go any further. There was a car parked at that ramp.

He found a good spot in the deep woods, loosened his belt, and squatted down. He heard laughter and looked up. In front of him, squinting through the briars, he could see a man and a young girl. They were eating sandwiches about a hundred yards away. He watched the little girl pour some kind of drink into cups, passing one to the man.

"Now, that's the way to start a date," he thought. Autumn was coming and there were plenty of early fallen leaves. He wiped with some of them and pulled up his pants. He stood to leave, but the girl's laughter gave him pause. He wanted to watch some more. Teg tossed his pile of shit aside with a stick and buried it with dirt and leaves. He needed this spot. He spread fresh leaves where he had toileted so he could sit there and watch through the briars.

The girl was lovely and he was intrigued. Teg pulled cheese crackers from his pocket and opened them. Never taking his eyes off of the girl or the man, he ate the crackers, throwing the wrapper aside. Overhead, the clouds thickened. Teg didn't look up. He was transfixed by the little blond girl.

The little girl was drawing or writing in a tablet of some kind. The man lay down on his back on a blanket. Teg licked his lips. He couldn't hear their conversation. Soon enough, he could tell the man had fallen asleep. He could see the chest rising and falling rhythmically. If not . . . if the man was awake, he'd be happy to make his slumber permanent.

Teg stepped onto the path towards the girl. She had her back to him near the river. He moved closer, behind a tree and watched as the wind caught her drawing pad and blew it from her hand. She ran and scooped it up and put it in her backpack. Then she put her arms through, swinging the pack around to her back like a camper. The child moved back to the river. She was talking to a squirrel sitting on a rock on the river bank.

"Hey, little squirrel. Did you drop your acorn? There's another one over there. Go get it. Get it, little squirrel."

Teg sprinted like a panther and scooped her up quickly, hand over her mouth. She kicked him hard and struggled as he walked fast up the trail. It would be a hike to get to his car. Cara tried hard to scream for her daddy, but she couldn't make a sound.

When they were far enough away, Teg said, "You're a real fighter aren't you little girl?"

She bit the fleshy part of his hand. Teg just laughed. He liked the pain.

They reached the other boat ramp and the SUV, a long way away from the picnic spot. Teg let go of her mouth and opened the passenger door. He pulled her backpack off and tossed it in the backseat. Holding Cara with one hand, he attempted to buckle her in. She screamed loud, but no one was around to hear her. The little girl was a fighter and she was quick. She darted under her captor's arm and ran towards the ramp. Teg laughed and chased after her.

"Come back here, pretty girl. I ain't gonna hurt you none."

Cara dived off the ramp and into the icy water. The water was unexpected, not like a bath or a swimming pool . . . freezing . . .

shocking . . . She struggled to stay afloat, to swim. Her foot was caught on something . . . pulling her down . . . she couldn't breathe . . . She needed her daddy.

CHAPTER 24
AFTER DINNER

Pam and I took Melanie's dog, Molly, for a walk while Lizzie and Lois helped Melanie clean up the kitchen. The rest of the girls were back in the workroom finishing their fairy houses. Sweet Emily and Kyra surprised us later by repairing the damage to Pam's and my squooshed clay houses. I love those girls.

We walked down the sidewalk near the Carrollton Police station with Molly leading the way. Walking Molly was a favorite task that all the girls in the studio helped with.

A police car pulled up next to us and the window rolled down. I recognized Chad Milner's handsome face. He's a sweetheart.

"Lord! There's two of you!" he said, laughing.

"Hey, Chad. This is my twin sister, Pam."

Pam perked right up at the sight of the officer. She's such a cougar.

"Hi, there. Nice to meet you, Chad."

Chad leaned out the window. "Hey, Molly."

Melanie's short haired little rescue dog gave him a friendly bark in reply.

"How are you, Penny?"

"I'm sparkling, Chad. It's good to see you."

"You ladies working at the Blue Heron tonight?"

"We are."

Pam said, "We've been talking about that missing girl, Cara. The one they think drowned in the Little Tallapoosa."

"Wasn't that something? So sad. I've been assigned that case. We've had to look in spits and spurts because of all the flooding in the area."

"Is there any thought that the father might have done something to her?"

Chad looked surprised at my sister's question. "I can't really discuss that, other than to say that we are looking at everything and everyone."

"Are you still looking for her?" I asked. Might as well. Pam's never going to let up.

Chad looked solemn. "We won't stop until we find her. Her body will probably turn up somewhere, maybe when the river's down again. The official search has been suspended due to the heavy rains. Still, I go out there when I can. And volunteers are looking, too."

"We could help look," Pam said.

Chad seemed surprised. "Well, sure. You ladies want to take your walks on the river, go right ahead." He grinned. "Watch out for snakes, though. We must have killed twenty or so along those banks while we were out there. But you go right ahead. Give me a call if you find anything or need me to send an EMT with a snakebite kit."

"I think we'll leave the search to professionals," I said. I had no intention of slogging around in snake flooded terrain. Not now. Not ever.

CHAPTER 25
NOT TODAY

Straddling two boulders, Teg reached down into the frigid water and pulled Cara up by her hair. Her skin was bluish and she wasn't breathing. He'd kill her soon enough, but they hadn't had a proper date yet. He wasn't ready for her to die. Not this way.

He laid her on the bank and pulled her sparkly pink shirt over her head and slung it aside. It caught on a low tree branch and hung there, waving in the wind.

Teg compressed Cara's chest with both hands, the way he'd been taught in the Prison First Aid class. A few compressions, and she gasped, vomiting up water. He turned her on her side allowing her to expel the rest.

He had to undo a Velcro strap and wiggle her rain boot to get it off her foot. It was filled with water. He emptied it out and shook it good. While Cara gasped for breath, Teg walked to the river edge and looked for the other boot, but he couldn't find it. He walked back to the child. She was coughing and gasping. She'd be okay.

Cara was cold and exhausted as Teg picked her up and carried her to the car. The fight was gone for now. He threw the boot in the back seat next to her backpack. She didn't struggle at all as he put the seat belt around her. Her teeth were chattering, her skin still blue. Cara gasped to fill her lungs with precious air. Teg shut the door and walked around to the driver's side. He didn't bother with his own seat belt. Instead, he reached back and picked up the backpack. He looked in and found, next to a drawing pad, a white t-shirt with a pink unicorn on the front. He handed the shirt to Cara and put the backpack in the floorboard at her feet. With shaking hands, Cara pulled the shirt over her head, maneuvering it around the seatbelt. Her pants were soaked and she was still cold.

"Sorry I ain't got no blanket for you. You'll warm up soon enough." Teg turned the heater on high and directed all the vents her way.

It had begun to rain. Teg turned on the wipers, pulled out of the small parking lot, and headed west on the back roads toward Tallapoosa.

CHAPTER 26
SHE DID IT AGAIN

My cell phone rang at 8:00 a.m., waking me up. It had to be my mother. Nobody ever calls this early except for her. I looked over at Dan's side of the bed. He was gone. I remembered that he had a morning meeting at the university. I looked at my phone and sat up in the bed. It was Lizzie calling.

"Hey. What's wrong?"

"Morning, Penny. Nothing's wrong. Do you want to meet at my house or should I come there?"

"What are you talking about?"

"The search for the little girl. Pam called last night and said you needed help."

Pam opened my bedroom door and flipped my light on. She was fully dressed and sipping a cup of coffee. She had a second cup in her left hand, I assume for me.

"Hang on a second, Lizzie." I didn't bother muting the phone. I wanted her to hear what I said to my sister.

"Morning," Pam said. "Is that Lizzie on the phone?"

"It is."

"She wants to hang out with us?"

"Um no. She wants to go on a hunt with us. You know anything about that?"

"I never said anything about a hunt. I just thought we could go have some fun together. Eat lunch at the Corner Café."

"When you lie you take straw out of the baby Jesus' manger. It's gonna be a cold winter and if the baby Jesus shivers it'll be your fault."

I could hear Lizzie laughing. "Penny, C'mon. I need an adventure."

Pam added, "All we want to do is talk to Cara's dad. That's all. Then we will let it go."

"Okay, that's even more straw out of the manger. Poor, poor baby Jesus. You don't know how to let anything go."

I could hear Lizzie yelling "Penny, PENNY! Talk to me."

"What is it Lizzie?" I refused Pam's offer of coffee. I'd get my own, thank you very much.

Lizzie said, "I found Leman's phone number and called him last night. He's got a few minutes before he has to meet with detectives at nine. He's very grateful that you agreed to talk to him. So get up and get dressed, I'm on my way to your house. And hurry. He's waiting."

"I'm going to kill both of you. When we get to the Corner Café, be sure to order the spinach artichoke dip. I think a tablespoon of arsenic will blend in nicely."

"Sorry, no arsenic for me. I have a dental appointment." Lizzie was still laughing as I hung up on her.

I pushed Pam out of my room, shut my door, and turned on the shower.

CHAPTER 27
WHAT'S THE PASSWORD?

Teg stuck to roads along the rivers. He liked the views and there was little traffic. He passed a couple of police cars, but they didn't come after him. His heart would pound when he'd spot a trooper and he couldn't figure out for the life of him why there wasn't a report out on the SUV. Whatever . . . he wasn't gonna complain about it.

He looked over at Cara. Her teeth were chattering. She was dry now so he didn't know why. He still had the heat on and it was stifling hot. She looked terrified, so maybe that caused her to be cold. He really needed to have a date with her soon.

"That man you was with . . . that your daddy?"

"Yes."

"You having a date with him?"

She had no idea what he meant by that. "We were having a picnic. Take me back there right now."

"Don't get all lippy with me, little girl. After I saved your life and all . . . you could have drowned."

And then the flood gates came. Cara cried loud sobbing tears, something she hardly ever did.

Teg reached over and patted her arm.

"Shhh, it's okay. Your daddy asked me to pick you up. He was really tired and wanted me to take you somewhere else. Somewhere more fun. He didn't want you to get caught out in the rain."

Cara knew that was a big fat lie. Through her sobs, she said, "No, he didn't."

"He did. He called me at work and asked me to come down there. Called me on this."

He pulled out the cell phone he'd taken from Voncille and laid it on the console.

She squinted her eyes at the phone and then glared at Teg. "If my daddy sent you, what's the password?"

Cara knew all about stranger danger. She'd learned about it at Carrollton Elementary School and she and her father had discussed it several times. They even had a password: *"County Fair."* And all this school year, they had practiced using it.

Leman picked Cara up every day from school, sitting in the long car line waiting on his daughter. He had warned Cara that if anyone ever showed up there other than him, even if they had the sign in the window with her name, they had to say *"County Fair"* before she was to get in the car. He told her that they would practice this and to be on guard for strangers.

A few days later, Leman arrived at the school dressed as Batman. Cara knew full well that it was her daddy. She walked to the car, to the lowered window and asked him, "What's the Password?"

Batman said, "Ummm, Pencil Sharpener."

"Wrong." She giggled and then made a serious face.

"Hamburger with onions."

More laughter, "Nope."

"County Fair!"

"Hi, Daddy."

Cara hopped in the backseat of the car. The teachers on car duty thought the whole thing charming.

A few weeks later, Leman showed up dressed as an old lady; another time, a dinosaur. And each time, Cara would refuse to get in the car until he said, "County Fair."

Teg looked over at Cara. "Password? I'm supposed to know a password?"

Cara, still sobbing, nodded.

He looked at her shirt, "Unicorn?"

She shook her head no and, defiantly, crossed her arms across her chest.

"Pizza!"

"NO"

"Teddy Bear."

"NO, and YOU ARE a STRANGER!!!"

"Okay, little smart girl. I'll give you that. I AM a stranger. But that don't mean I'm a bad stranger. Some strangers are good strangers."

Cara looked out the window and said softly, hiccupping through her tears, "No, they aren't."

CHAPTER 28
LEMAN'S HOUSE

I was surprised at how close I lived to Leman Garrett. His house sat a little over two miles away over on Cedar Street. The house was charming. It was built, probably in the 1930s like other houses on the street. The home was made of wood sitting on a brick foundation. The clapboard siding was painted white with black shutters. The front door was a dark green. Hanging baskets hung from the front porch, and a pink sparkly bicycle leaned against the railing. A sidewalk and bike lane stretched along shady Cedar Street, making it easy for residents to walk or bike up to Adamson Square. It is a lovely place to raise a child.

Lizzie knocked on the door and Leman welcomed her, Pam, and me into the house. I was immediately struck by all of the paintings that hung on the walls. The artist had a rare gift. There were also several drawings and paintings clearly done by a child. They were also very well done.

Leman said, "Those paintings were done by my wife, Julie. She passed away from cancer when Cara was two."

"I'm so sorry to hear that," I said. I already knew the story from the newspaper articles about the missing child. "Are these others . . . are they Cara's?"

He nodded. "She's going to be an artist like her mom."

Lizzie observed, "Looks like she already is. We want to help you find her, Leman. Whatever we can do."

"I just made you ladies some coffee."

We followed Leman to the kitchen where he began pouring us cups of hot, rich, black coffee. I can't drink it black but didn't want to ask for anything, so I pretended to sip.

I saw a little license plate next to a Walmart bag on the kitchen table on top of yesterday's newspaper and sat my cup next to it. It was the kind of tag kids put on the back of their bikes. A tiny bottle of black enamel paint from a model car set was open nearby with a small paintbrush sticking out of the top. I could tell Leman was trying to change the tag from "*LARA*" to "*CARA*." A black spotted towel and the smell of mineral spirits proved his many unsuccessful attempts. I looked back at the tag. You could tell that his strokes were made with a shaking hand. I expect this project was what had brought Leman to Walmart when I first met him.

"Do you mind if I try, Leman?" I gestured at the project.

He looked relieved. "Please! If you don't mind."

I sat at the table and used the mineral spirit soaked towel to wipe away the paint. Then I picked up the brush. Pam and Lizzie sat across from me while Leman leaned on the kitchen counter to my right, watching me paint.

Pam had promised me in the drive over not to mention her dreams to Leman. She asked, "Why are you so sure that she didn't drown?"

Leman paused for a moment. "She called me."

I looked up from the tag and we all gasped.

"It was early in the morning on the third day she was gone. I hadn't slept in 48 hours and had drifted off on the sofa."

He looked embarrassed that he had dared sleep with his child missing. I couldn't imagine his exhaustion.

Leman continued. "I was just waking up when the house phone rang. I don't know why I still have one. No one ever calls it anymore except politicians and folks selling stuff."

We all nodded at this universal problem.

He repeated, "I heard the phone ringing. It took a minute for me to register that's what I was hearing because we only have one land line phone and it's in the kitchen, I walked in here and answered it and I heard her little voice."

Leman's voice broke then and his eyes filled with tears.

Lizzie stood up and touched his arm. "What did she say?"

"She said, 'Daddy help me. I'm scared. I don't know where I am.' And then the phone went dead. I tried to do that thing where you dial 611 and try to find the number that called you, but it didn't work. I called the police, but they couldn't trace it. They just think I'm crazy and that I made it all up or dreamed it."

That's what I thought, too. I had finished painting the tag and screwed the lid on the paint bottle. I was thinking that the poor man in his grief, probably did imagine the whole thing. So I asked gently, "And you're sure it wasn't a dream, Leman?"

"No. It wasn't a dream. I've now got the house phone forwarded to my cell phone just in case she calls me back and I'm not here. She always forgets my cell number."

I should have known better than to ask if it was a dream because it opened the door for Pam to say, "I'm the one who dreams, Leman. I see her alive in mine. We'll help you find her."

CHAPTER 29
WHAT'S IN A NAME?

Maple Street became Highway 166 and took them through Bowdon. Teg turned left onto Wedowee Street/GA 100 and then straight onto W Highway 5. Teg saw the state line sign as they crossed over into Alabama. From a piece of paper in his lap, he consulted the scribbled directions he had put together at the motel, just in case, and was assured he was going the right way. The road became Highway 48. A con at the state prison had told him about a hunting cabin he would go to with some buddies somewhere around here. He remembered it was near a town named Graham. He wondered if he could find the cabin, or an abandoned one like it. Road signs pointed him up County Road 87 and he made the turn.

He could see a good number of creek tributaries that connected to the Little Tallapoosa. It sure was a pretty place. Lots of woods around . . . lots of privacy . . . and slightly elevated in contrast with the flat land he'd been driving through.

"What's your name, little girl?"

She continued looking out the window. "Cara Louise."

"Pretty name. Mine's Teg."

Cara squinted her eyes the way she always did when she heard a lie. "That's not a name. You're a liar."

Teg chuckled. He reached in his pocket and tossed her his wallet. Look for yourself. Teg's my nickname. Everyone calls me that, even my daddy."

Cara looked in the wallet. It had money in it and she found an ID that said, "Thomas Granger Duke."

Cara didn't say a word, but she thought about what she would write in her journal later. She did this often. Work out the words in her head . . . whole paragraphs . . . and then when she had it the way she wanted it, she would write it down. Composing for her journal helped Cara separate, at least for the moment, from her fear. She looked out the window and closed her eyes, composing.

Duke? Thats a name for a dog. My great Aunt Nettie used to have a dog named Duke. Daddy said she named all her old dogs the same thing. He said shes had about 50 dogs all of em named Duke. Me and Daddy visited her in a trailer park in Tennessee once. I didn't like her at all. She pinched my cheeks and said nasty things I didnt understand about my Mama. She told Daddy that Mama died because she slept with boys when she was a tenager and that caused her cancer.

This girl in my class named Lisa has 4 brothers. I'm glad she has her on room and dont have to sleep with her brothers so that way she wont get the cancer.

My Daddy got mad and yelled at Aunt Nettie for saying that about my mama. And then he said that we were leaving. And we did! I was glad cause shes really mean. And I didn't like her old dog either. He stunk. Just like this mean man.

Teg looked out his own side window. The SUV was climbing now, above the creek that ran fifty feet or so below him to his left, the craggy mountain to the right. He read the green sign on the edge of the road. Shoal Creek. He remembered the con, Elvin, had said something about Shoal Creek. He needed to watch for dirt roads that would take him up the mountain off the main road. It would be hit or miss finding the cabin as he didn't have directions. The rain was coming down hard now and he adjusted the wipers to full speed.

"Hey. You asleep? Give me back my wallet, girl."

Cara put the ID back in the wallet and threw it in the floor.

Annoyed, Teg turned to her and reached over with the back of his hand and smacked her hard across the cheek. "You be nice now. You hear me?"

No one had ever hit Cara before. Not even a classmate . . . and certainly not her father.

She was warm now, hot actually. Enraged, she turned her body, still seat belted, towards Teg and began kicking. She kicked hard. She had a yellow belt in Karate. Cara knew how to kick. Her blows landed hard on his right arm.

"**DON'T . . . YOU . . . HIT . . . ME!**" She screamed.

Teg was caught off guard by the blows. He threw his arm up to block her feet.

"What the hell!" He looked at Cara, laughing, as she continued to kick with her tiny feet. "Got me a fighter."

Eyes on the child and off the road, Teg didn't see the curve ahead. The road cut right through the mountain, rock jutted out, here and there, on both sides almost making a tunnel. He drifted to the left side of the road and banged against the rock. Past the rock now, the driver side wheels of the big car slid in the loose asphalt on the shoulder. He tried to correct, jerking the steering wheel to the right, but it was too late. The greased slick wet road refused to provide traction to the SUV's big tires and they began spinning out of control. Cara closed her eyes and screamed. The earth gave way beneath them and the car plummeted down the rocky ravine.

CHAPTER 30
MAGNET WAR

Lizzie dropped us back at the house and hurried off to a dental appointment. She would be back after lunch. I was now resigned to the fact that she and Pam were involving me in a pointless investigation, and there was just nothing I could do about it.

Sneering at my old fashioned percolator, Pam made a pot of coffee, while I undid Dan's dirty deed of the morning.

Friends and family think Dan and I have this perfect marriage. And I admit, we pretty much do, but we also have our little battles. One of those battles has been going on for two years, ever since we bought the new stainless steel refrigerator. Just like my new fancy microwave, I love that appliance. I keep it gleaming with Sparkle Shine and I don't let lettuce or Vidalia onions rot in the crisper like I'd been known to do in the past.

When we were making the purchase at Home Depot, I spotted a display of awesome refrigerator magnets and just had to have one.

The magnet is actually a clay pot. It came with a tiny aloe plant that grew in real dirt and moss. The double magnets on the back of the light grey on dark grey striped pot were very strong, assuring it would stay where it was placed.

At the time, Dan scoffed, "Why in the world are you buying that ugly thing?"

"It's beautiful, and it will look fantastic on the front of the fridge. I'm tired of all the cheap magnets we had stuck all over the old fridge. Why do we need to advertise tow trucks and pizza restaurants right in our kitchen?"

"It's a great way to find their numbers when you've set off the fire alarm cooking dinner, or blown a tire driving over pottery shards at the Blue Heron."

He thinks he's so funny.

"I hate them. I've hated them for a long, long time. They make our kitchen look tacky."

"I had no idea that this was such a huge source of stress for you."

"Well, it is. I've already thrown the old magnets out. On the front of our new stainless steel refrigerator will live this beautiful little plant in its beautiful pot and it shall be the only adornment ever to be placed there."

Dan rolled his eyes. "You do realize that you will kill that plant like you do every single living plant you bring into the house."

"Not this one. It will be in the kitchen, right across from the sink, where I can remember to water it."

Two weeks later the plant was shriveled up and dead. I was horrified. Before Dan got home from work, I drove to Hobby Lobby, and thankfully, found a plastic plant that looked similar. I swapped out the dead one. Dan would never notice.

And, he didn't, because, when he was in the kitchen, I pretended to mist it. But, that didn't stop the magnet war. The pot sticks out a good three inches from the refrigerator door and Dan tends . . . deliberately if you ask me . . . to brush it as he walks by. So just out of pure meanness, he takes it off and sticks the pot magnet to the side of the refrigerator, out of sight.

And every time I walk in the kitchen, I spot two little circles where the magnets were, disturbing the gleam of the stainless steel. I remove the pot from the side of the fridge and put it right back, carefully aligning the magnets over the two circles. Then I take my Sparkle Shine and polish off the two circles from the side.

This magnet moving war happens several times a day, and it has gone on, with no discussion whatsoever, for two whole years. He will never win.

Pam watched this process, "I can't believe you've kept that plant alive."

AHA! I'd fooled her too.

She handed me a cup of coffee. "I assumed . . . knowing you . . . that you'd kill plastic plants the same as you do real ones. And seriously, get a new coffee pot."

CHAPTER 31
CRASH

The SUV hit hard, fifty feet below the road against large rocks that jutted out of the deep and narrow ravine. The driver's side front panel took most of the blow, crushing the front of the vehicle like an accordion, driving the steering wheel into Teg's gut. His legs were pushed up by the crumpling floor board, snapping both tibias. The front window spider webbed in front of him, but it didn't fully break. A young pine tree below, just beginning to mature, pierced the engine, and slid under the steering wheel puncturing just below Teg's belt into his groin. He screamed as blood bubbled up his throat and trickled out the corner of his mouth. An added insult, the airbag exploded in his face, leaving a dusting of white powder.

Cara was tilted sideways, but she was held in place by her seat belt. The thud took the breath out of her as the SUV hit the rocks. Her airbag exploded, as well. It hurt something awful. But she was uninjured, save for seatbelt burns across her chest, some bruises as her shoulder slammed into the door, and a bloody nose from the airbag.

The SUV teetered and then settled into place, wedged on both sides in the narrow rocky crevice of the ravine. All four wheels were suspended about three feet from the little creek below. The young pine tree, impaling Teg, bowed under the stress of it all and finally snapped in two near its roots.

CHAPTER 32
THE LITTLE TALLAPOOSA

Lizzie arrived later, her wavy red hair in disarray, and pink lipstick smudged around her mouth. Poor thing was all numbed up with Novocain. I gave her some iced tea just to watch it dribble out the side of her mouth. She's my closest friend in Carrollton, so I have that right.

I asked her if she wanted to wait for the numbing effect to wear off, but she was raring to get started, I think, because she said, "Eh go."

I drove over to the Tallapoosa River, parking close to the boat ramp. Leman had given us directions to follow to find his and Cara's picnic spot. He told me to park at the second ramp. The first one was much further away, and a good hike to the picnic spot. The second, only a few hundred feet away.

He had told us, that the last time he saw Cara, she was sitting on the blanket sketching pictures. He'd watched her for a while and dozed off, something he would regret for the rest of his life.

Leman had said, "When I woke up, my little girl was gone. I yelled as loud as I could, and I looked everywhere for her. There were footprints, too, down by the river's edge. Little footprints of Cara's, but also some big shoe impressions, like a grown man . . . not mine. They got washed away in the rain before the police finally got there. And, I don't think they believed me."

Pam asked him, "Why not?"

"During the interview, I could tell that the officers were sympathetic . . . didn't want me blaming myself for falling asleep. I think they thought I imagined the shoeprints to take away my own guilt. They said as much to me. . . . I know what I saw. And if someone got her while I was sleeping and not watching . . . that's worse than drowning." His eyes filled with tears. "And some of their questions, a lot of them . . . like I had maybe done something terrible to her. You know what I mean?"

What could we say? It was a terrible thing and none of us believed for one second, that this father had done anything to his little girl. Lizzie asked him if we could see Cara's sketchbook.

"No. It was gone, too. So was her backpack. They found her little shirt, but they've never found the backpack with her drawing stuff and they've never found her. Please help me."

And so, we were doing just that, futile as it was. We followed the hand drawn map and found the area Leman had described. It was very close to the ramp and a pretty spot. All three of us could picture the blanket spread among the leaves with the sandwiches and Kool-Aid . . . father and daughter enjoying a beautiful day . . . a picnic on the river.

We followed the river's flow downstream and walked along the edge. Some areas were thick with briars and brambles. Pam took care of those with her switchblade. I could tell Lizzie was shocked that Pam owned such a thing. But, not me. I've seen it before, not too long ago, in a much scarier situation.

We had walked in single file about a half mile, our shoes coated in sticky mud. Lizzie had moved in front of Pam. Suddenly she stopped.

"Ake . . . ake . . . ake."

"Your feet are aching? Do you need to stop and rest, Lizzie?" I asked from the back. Looking at the mud, I knew there was no place to sit down.

Pam said, "I think she's saying snake. You saying snake, Lizzie?"

"Ake!"

Pam pulled Lizzie back and stepped forward. I leaned over Pam's shoulder. A large water moccasin . . . some folks around here call them cottonmouths . . . at least four feet in length and a good five inches in diameter, sat curled on the path, its tongue flickering in our direction.

Pam held up the knife, the blade aiming down at the venomous snake.

I whispered in Pam's ear. "Don't even think about it. He's in striking distance and you are not Crocodile Dundee. Lizzie, step back some more."

I could feel her move about five feet behind me. I whispered to Pam. "Keep your arms still. Don't move that knife. And very slowly, step back."

She did as I said, for once in her life. All three of us continued slowly moving back until we were safe and then we hightailed it to the car. We were done for the day.

"Ake ooo," said Lizzie when we turned back onto the highway.

"You're very welcome, Lizzie."

CHAPTER 33
DOORS AND WINDOWS

Cara unbuckled her seatbelt and wiped the blood from her nose on the hem of her shirt. She looked over at Teg. He looked awful. His skin was grey-like. He was moaning and she could see blood on his mouth and blood pooled in his lap where a piece of tree had impaled him.

Cara found the button that unlocked the car's doors. She grabbed the handle and tried to open her door but, wedged against the rocks, it wouldn't budge. She climbed over the console, into the backseat, moving quickly, before the Duke man could grab her. She tried the passenger door first. It was stuck like the front seat door. She scooted over behind Teg, and tried that one. It opened several inches before hitting rock. Looking down, through the open crack, Cara could see the creek flowing under her. She lay on her stomach and stretched her fingers down toward the water, but it was beyond her reach. So, instead, she held her fingers out at the rocks, catching a little rainwater. She allowed the door to close and sucked the water off her fingers.

She tried all of the windows. None worked. She didn't know it, but the fuse that controlled them had blown in the crash. And, the windows would do no good if opened, anyway. She would never be able to climb the rocks that surrounded her. No way out. Her daddy would have to find her.

The rain was pouring down in deafening cascades. Cara lay down in the back seat. She began crying again. She cried and cried until she finally drifted off to sleep.

In the front, Teg was unconscious, but still alive . . . barely. Blood seeped slowly from the wound below his belly. Oddly, the tree that impaled him, pressed on arteries and prevented him from completely bleeding out. He dreamed.

CHAPTER 34
SOMETHING'S COMING

"Hey, Mom." It was seven in the morning, my mother's normal calling time.

"I thought I'd catch you before you got off and running for the day. You're always so busy."

I don't know where or what my mother thinks I go and do that early in the morning.

We chatted about Pam's visit, and I told her about our adventures from the day before. Then, just when I had her stirred up over the possibility of snake attacks, I changed the subject.

"How's your restless leg problem? You still taking the Requip?"

Mom's legs give her fits at night and her doctor had prescribed a medication to help with the problem.

"It's helped some. We'll see."

"You bought any tickets to Vegas?"

"No, Smarty."

"Lottery tickets? You hitting up the convenience stores?"

"You sound like your sister. Pam asked me the same thing."

One of the side effects listed on Mom's Requip was, "May cause an urge to gamble." Pam and I thought this was just hilarious. So we question her all the time to make sure she hasn't blown her life savings.

"Penny," she said, changing the subject, "Your brother's a little mad at you."

"What for? I haven't talked to Brett in days."

"Mmm Hmm. Well, you should. That may be part of it. He says you and Pam have gone and gotten all famous because of Jacey's case and you left him out. He says you should have let him help. He knows more about anatomy than you do, him being a nurse and a snake handler and all."

"What in the world does that have to do with anything? It's been a year. I had no idea he was holding a grudge."

"Well, it was a decapitation, wasn't it? That kind of thing is right up his alley."

"Really? My brother is a decapitation expert. Who knew?"

"I don't think that's what he meant. But he did once dissect a squirrel that's head had been bitten off by a mountain lion. He had it in his freezer for months. Finally thawed it out in his microwave and fed the thing to his python."

"Speaking of pythons, you will recall that when Pam and I were in Tennessee investigating Jacey's murder charges, Brett was dealing with a tumor on the belly of Julius Squeezer."

"Yes, I do remember that. He could have brought Julius with him."

She couldn't be serious!

"Mom, Julius is seventeen feet long. I'm pretty sure the motel we stayed at would have said, 'no'."

"Doesn't matter. His feelings are hurt."

This conversation was a little much for me this early in the morning and prior to coffee.

"I tell you what, Mom. I'll call him later and talk to him. Make peace."

"Don't bother. He just left his house. He's heading down there. I gave him Dan's chocolate chip pecan pie to bring. Tell Dan to warm it some in your new microwave. Cover it first with Saran Wrap. And then put some whipped cream on top before he eats it. I sent him a can of that, too."

"Brett's coming here? To Carrollton?"

"Yes. Pam called him. He's coming down there to help you find that little girl. Help you girls watch out for snakes, he said. Tell Dan that pie's all for him. Tell him the pecans came from Jim Sherby's tree. Remember that tree by the road? It was loaded with pecans this year. Dan will remember even if you don't. Brett helped me pick them up and crack them open. I only had to throw two or three out for rot. It's up to Dan whether he shares any pie with you and Pam. Tell Brett to call me when he gets there, so I know he got there okay."

My family is totally insane. All of them. Except for me, of course.

CHAPTER 35
DAY 2 – STRANDED

Cara awoke with the morning light, shivering and sore. Whiplash had set in and her little arms and neck hurt something awful. For a while, she was disoriented, trying to figure out where she was. And then she remembered. She sat up slowly and peered over the seat at the Duke man. His eyes were closed, his breathing ragged. He appeared to be asleep.

Cara could see her backpack under his legs. The dashboard of the car on that side was caved in and rested near the man's knees. Very carefully, Cara moved back to the front seat and into the floorboard. The dash on her side of the car wasn't damaged much.

She watched Teg for a few minutes. Then, as her courage grew, she moved her hand gingerly towards the backpack. Teg moaned and she snatched her hand back. She waited until he was quiet and then tried again. She wrapped her fingers around one of the straps and jerked it quickly towards her. She could feel the soreness in her shoulder as she did so, but Cara was determined to succeed. The movement lifted Teg's right knee, pushing it into the crumpled dash. He woke, screaming. His broken legs . . . hard shooting pain, excruciating. He passed out again.

The screams terrified Cara. She held her backpack against her chest and stayed on the floor board for several minutes. From where she was, she could see a glint of metal. She reached again.

Teg didn't wake this time, as Cara carefully slid the knife from the strap on his sock. It had a very large and scary, wicked blade. She threw the weapon into her backpack and climbed back over the console. Her daddy would be very upset when he found out she had taken the knife. She wasn't allowed to use anything but a butter knife at home. She hoped he would understand.

From the back seat, she examined the wide sharp blade. It looked very dangerous. Cara decided the safest place for it was the pocket on the back of the seat and so she placed it there with the handle sticking out.

Hungry, she looked through her backpack, but all the food from the picnic was back at the river.

She climbed further into the back of the SUV. Like the doors, the hatch wouldn't open, either. Cara found the grocery sacks of food and dug through them for something she could eat. There was a half a loaf of stale bread and a jar of peanut butter and a good number of canned goods.

Cara decided to dip the bread into the jar, rather than risk using the sharp knife. Her belly full of peanut butter and bread, she opened the door again and reached out for more rainwater.

Cara had put off her most pressing need and she couldn't wait any longer. She really, really had to pee. She moved behind Teg, so that if he woke up, he wouldn't be able to see. She took off her pants and panties and held one of the plastic grocery bags between her legs.

"This is so gross," she said, as some of her urine got on her hands. When she was finished, she pushed the bag through the crack in the door and let it go, watching it drop to the creek below.

"I'm a litterer," she said, sadly.

She might be here all day before someone found her and she might need to go again. So, Cara decided that, when that time came, she would empty the bag of just pee into the creek. She would store the bag somewhere to use again.

Cara washed her hands in the heavy, pouring rain.

CHAPTER 36
SNAKE EXPERT

Dan called from the golf course and I broke the news to him that Brett was coming and confessed the whole reason behind it.

"I can't believe you are doing this. Didn't you have enough excitement in Tennessee?" He sounded somewhat stern.

"It's not my fault. Blame Pam and Lizzie. For that matter, blame my mom. By the way, she's sending you pie."

"What kind of pie."

"Chocolate chip pecan. She told me to tell you to eat it warm with whipped cream and that she gathered all of the nuts herself from Jim Sherby's yard."

"Chocolate chip pecan, huh?" Dan was beginning to soften. "Don't you dare touch my pie."

Brett arrived around eleven with pie in tow. I made him and Pam a nice lunch, Mediterranean sandwiches on hollowed submarine missile bread, one of my new specialties. I sautéed chicken pieces with a little Teriyaki sauce. Then I drizzled the pan with a melted pesto that I made with fresh butter, basil and minced garlic. I combined all of that in a bowl with stuff I'd already marinated in vinegar and oil that included chopped fresh spinach, tomato, onion, pepperoni pieces, and Kalamata olives. Finally, I add asiago cheese and stuffed the mixture into the bread, which I'd hollowed out from the end so that you can hold them up and eat them without everything falling out.

"Oh, my word, Penny." Pam was visibly surprised. "Something extraordinary has happened to you ever since your microwave died. You are becoming quite the chef I must say."

My little brother loved it too, even asking for a second one. Might as well, Dan wasn't planning on sharing any pie with any of us.

While we ate, we filled Brett in on the little girl's disappearance, ending with our adventure with the water moccasin on the Little Tallapoosa.

"You don't want to mess with them," Brett said.

"We had no intention of MESSING with it. We left as soon as we could safely back away from the thing."

"And you are positive it was a water moccasin?"

"I'm positive," I said. "Why?"

"It's just that they would be rare in this part of Georgia. More than likely it's a Midland water snake. They look the same but the pattern is reversed. By the way, they're completely harmless."

I thought about all the snakes killed by searchers for the little girl that Chad had told us about. I winced a little and decided not to tell Brett that bit of news. He's sensitive about killing snakes unnecessarily.

A couple of years back, Brett was booked at a snake show in Charlotte, North Carolina. He attended these shows now and then to sell snake hooks he made from old golf clubs and a device that he created that showed snake breeders whether a snake is a male or female. Brett sold these devices online, too. To save money on a hotel, he had agreed to camp out as an overnight guard in the large gymnasium that was hosting the event.

Brett had collected and rescued snakes since he was a little boy. I don't know anyone who knows more about their habitats than my brother. At one time, he owned fifty-five snakes. My mother was terrified of them, but I didn't mind them as long as they were nonvenomous or properly contained.

Brett arrived in Charlotte with a cold, and stopped and bought some Nyquil. After setting up his booth, he met the other participant guards who would, like him, be sleeping there that night. Brett wasn't feeling very well at all and was annoyed when he saw that his partners were actually a married couple with a small baby. The room was filled with dangerous reptiles and snakes and he didn't think that it was safe or appropriate at all. Plus, feeling sick as he did, he didn't want to listen to a crying baby all night, nor spread his germs. So, he set up his sleeping bag as far away from the couple as he could, drank his Nyquil, and went to sleep.

Groggy from the medicine, Brett was soon awakened by a crashing sound. He turned on his flashlight and spotted a large terrapin crawling near him. He got up and found its container and returned the animal where it belonged.

Back in his sleeping bag, he began nodding off again, when he heard a louder crash, followed by additional crashes, one after the other. He heard a male voice yelling that there were snakes loose. Someone turned on the overhead lights. There were small nonvenomous snakes crawling everywhere. Brett and the married couple ran around the gymnasium, gathering up the slippery snakes and returning them to their cases, making sure they latched the tops.

As Brett walked down one aisle, he realized what was happening. A rather large Burmese Python, approximately seventeen feet long and as big around as a telephone pole had escaped. Its case stood open and empty. The serpent was knocking over other cages and aquariums, freeing animals, as it moved through the displays. Brett had no idea where the python had gone. He found the couple to tell them what he'd discovered.

And then it occurred to my brother that the couple was a long way from their baby. He took off running to the area where they had been camping. The baby was sound asleep in a playpen and the huge python was halfway in, its large head moving towards the infant.

Brett, yelling for help, grabbed the snake and began pulling as hard as he could. The python responded by turning on Brett and coiling around him. Brett and the snake fell to the floor in a powerful, rolling struggle. As Brett tried to free himself, the python tightened its hold, crushing him, and continued to roll. They crashed into shelves of containers and Brett could see aquariums full of deadly scorpions overhead, ready to rain down on top of his balding head.

The other two guards arrived and found the tail and began unwrapping the serpent from my brother. When Brett was free, the python crawled into a set of bleachers where it remained all night.

There was no way any of them could safely go to sleep with the snake on the loose so they had to sit up the rest of the night and watch. Finally, the python crawled out and they were able to safely catch and contain it properly. Minutes later, the lights came on signaling the beginning of the show.

When the owners of the massive serpent heard the story, they realized they had a huge liability on their hands. And so, upon his request, they gave Brett the python. He brought it home and named it Julius Squeezer and over time, they became friends.

My brother knows about every kind of snake there is. I don't imagine we would care whether they are male or female, but it would be nice to know whether they were dangerous. So, if we were going to return to the banks of the Little Tallapoosa, I was glad to have Brett along.

CHAPTER 37
DAY 3

Cara spent her third day in the car, much as she had the day before. She ate the dry bread and peanut butter. Needing more water than she was getting off of her fingers, she squeezed the top of her rain boot through the crack and let the rain fill it up. Several times, she filled the boot and then poured it out until she felt it was as clean as she could get it. Then she filled it again, wrinkling her nose as she sipped the cool water. There was no smell or foul taste. Still, it was the thought of drinking from a boot that bothered her.

Teg moaned from the front seat.

"Help me," he said.

Cara froze.

"Please, help me."

She took the boot and leaned over the seat and held it to his stranger danger lips.

Looking down at him, Cara saw the cell phone in his shirt pocket.

She reached slowly down and slid the phone up with two fingers.

Teg grabbed her wrist and Cara squealed. The phone fell back into his pocket.

"I have to call someone to help you. Let go of me."

He did and she reached again. This time, Teg clawed weakly at her hand, but Cara held the phone tightly and was soon back in her seat behind him. She flipped open the phone. In the back of her sketchbook, she had the house number and her daddy's cell phone number. Smart as she was, memorizing phone numbers had always been a problem.

She called her house praying he would be there. She knew her daddy would call the police and then come and get her.

The phone rang and rang.

And then her daddy answered, sleepily. "Hello?"

"Daddy help me. I'm scared. I don't know where I am."

"Cara?"

The phone went dead. Though unused, it hadn't been charged in a week. Cara tried again and again, but it was no use. She burst into tears and lay on her back and began kicking the window with her bare feet. Despite her Karate training, her little girl size 10 feet couldn't make so much as a crack in the glass.

CHAPTER 38
BAD FEELING – GOOD PIE

I sat down at the kitchen table next to my husband. He had a large wedge of warmed chocolate chip pecan pie with whipped topping and was slowly savoring every bite. I was relieved to see a piece of Saran Wrap next to my new microwave. Pam and Brett were outside on the screened porch pestering Roxie with a piece of string.

I said, "I want you to know that this isn't like the situation in Tennessee. We aren't going to be confronting any bad guys. This little girl probably drowned like the police say. We are just trying to help her father. And I doubt we'll be able to do that. But as a mom I just have to try."

Dan picked up a piece of the pie on his fork and held it to my lips.

"Mmm. Yum."

"I should have had a bad feeling last year when you went to Athens. I should have known you were in danger. But I had no idea. That bothers me. Just promise me you will be careful.

"I love you, too, Dan. And I do promise."

He kissed my lips and shared more pie with me. He's a generous, loving man.

"Promise me something else," he said.

"What's that?" I asked, my mouth full of rich chocolate and pecans.

"Promise me that you will never get this recipe from your mom."

I laughed. "Why not?"

"Because, by the time you and your brother and sister get back, I will have devoured this entire thing."

CHAPTER 39
DAY 4

Cara journaled and sketched in her book. The peanut butter was getting low and she would have to figure out a way to open some of the cans in the grocery bags. Lunch had been a small pack of cheese crackers. There was another pack left that she could eat for dinner. She sure wished she had a navel orange. She began sketching a bowl of fruit, shading each grape that hung over the side. Underneath that she wrote:

Daddy please save me an orange and some grapes. I miss you.

She heard a noise and looked up. Teg was shivering violently. There were no blankets in the car. Cara tried to go back to her writing.

The man in the front seat, the Duke man is cold. I dont have a

Cara didn't finish the sentence. Instead, she pulled the knife from the storage pocket and dropped it into the front passenger seat. She crawled over and into the floor board. With her back to the dash, she began carefully cutting the upholstery. The knife was huge and she was extra careful with it, holding the handle as tightly as she could manage.

Her shoulders and neck had loosened up since the accident, the soreness gone. Cara was able to cut a fairly big square from the seat and a bigger rectangle of fabric from the seat back. She placed these over Teg. Then she began pulling on the foam, using the knife to cut where she had to. Cara packed the golden foam material around Teg.

"Thank you," he whispered.

Cara didn't answer, but returned with the knife to her seat in back.

CHAPTER 40
SPIC N SPAN

A dried nugget of Spic n Span sits in my kitchen window. It's been there a long time . . . over two years. Dan's never noticed it, I don't think. Or if he did, he hasn't mentioned it. If he ever does, I'd probably tell him it's art and he'd say, "Oh, okay, then." My friends sometimes ask about it and I make up different stories. "It's from the bottom of the box and the recycling was due to go to the curb. Waste not. Want not." Or, "I keep it there to remind me to buy Spic n Span when I go to the store." Fact is, I don't know why it's there.

I was mopping the day that I got the call that my dad was being taken off the ventilator. He had been airlifted from Blue Ridge to Rome two months prior, near where Pam lives. MRSA had infected his heart and he needed specialized care. I commuted back and forth as much as I could over the next two months. Mom slept in Pam's guest room and I took the couch. I had driven home that morning to see Dan and get fresh clothes.

I hurried to finish the chore, and to put everything away so that I could race back to Rome . . . to Redmond Hospital . . . to the Intensive Care Unit. Pam and Mom and I were with Dad as he passed. We held his hands in ours, grieving together. Brett was in Blue Ridge at the time building a handicap ramp, still hoping our father would get better. I've known for some time that it bothered Brett that he wasn't there with us. And I'm sorry for that, too. I also know that my dad would have loved and approved of Brett's craftsmanship of the ramp.

Days later, after the funeral, I found the Spic n Span nugget in the corner of the kitchen, sitting there alone and crystalized. I put it in the window next to my dad's eyeglasses. I had found them, too, in my pocket the same day. Completely forgotten, they had been given to me by an ICU nurse before she covered my dad's face with a sheet.

Brett picked up the Spic n Span and then put it back. Then he picked up the glasses. "These Dad's?"

"Yep."

He put the glasses back where he found them. "Pam ready yet?"

I knocked on the guest room door. Time to head back to the Little Tallapoosa. Lizzie had to work so she wouldn't be joining us this time. At least that was her excuse. I think she'd had enough of snakes.

We showed Brett the picnic spot. He walked to the edge of the river, still swelling from the heavy rains of the last month. Then he walked back to where the blanket had been.

"It seems hard for me to believe that little girl would have walked into the river to wade without her daddy. The water is freezing cold."

I hadn't thought of that. "Not even with rain boots on?"

"You are a mom. If your child stepped into these waters to wade, they wouldn't have done it quietly. Wouldn't you wake up?"

"Yep. They would have squealed from the cold water. I would have heard them and woken up."

Pam agreed. "Any child would and any parent would."

Brett said, "But what if someone sneaked up behind her and grabbed her? Covered her mouth? You said there were footprints of an adult, right?"

"Well, that's what Leman said he saw. The rain had started soon after he woke up. If they were there, they'd been washed away by the time the police came." I was seeing the possibility, but still skeptical.

Pam said, "But no car. Leman would have woke up if he'd heard a car I would think. Or Cara would have woke him herself to let him know someone was there."

Brett turned away from the river and walked into the woods. We followed him.

We had walked a hundred yards or so, when Brett pointed. "Look there."

Another snake just like the one we had seen the day before, but a little smaller. Brett walked over and gently picked it up.

"Just as I thought. Midland water snake." He lay the snake on the ground and we watched it slither into the brambles.

A little further on, Brett stopped again. You could see a depression in the area and a piece of litter, a wrapper from a pack of cheese crackers.

"This wrapper could be from the searchers I guess." He sat down in the spot on the depression we had noticed. "When I sit here, through those briars, I can see that picnic spot. It's like looking through a camera lens or a telescope."

Following his lead, I sat down and looked. The brambles and briars were thick, but in the center they coiled together forming a sort of tube that ran all the way through. "You're right, Brett. I think someone could have sat here and watched them from behind. You've really got some good Indian hunting instincts."

Pam squatted next to me and looked through the tunnel as I had. I felt a chill and looked at Pam's arms. She had the same goose bumps standing up on hers.

She said, "If that's true. She may not be anywhere around here."

I drove us home, pondering what we'd discovered. "Why wouldn't the searchers or the police have seen what we did?"

Pam was thoughtful. "They believed she had drowned. I imagine their search was downstream, all along the river's edge and in the river itself. They found her shirt floating there didn't they?"

I shuddered, "If some pervert grabbed her. She's still probably dead."

"No she isn't," Pam said.

I didn't argue with her. Neither did Brett.

CHAPTER 41
DAY 5

Cara sat quietly in the backseat, sketching and journaling. She missed her school. At the beginning of the year, her first grade teacher had recommended her for the gifted class, mainly because of her advanced writing skills. She could compose sentences with a skill far beyond her classmates. Her spelling was superb for a six year old. Leman assumed this ability came from his wife. She, too, had been remarkably smart.

When he asked, Cara would give Teg water. Other than that, she tried her best to forget he was in the car. Concentrating on her sketch pad, she passed the time as well as she could.

When she got hungry, Cara scraped the last of the peanut butter with a spatula that she had made with a strip of the road map she had found in one of the storage pockets. She looked at it for a moment and then reached over and offered it to Teg. He shook his head, no.

"I can't," he said.

"You'll starve," she responded.

Teg chuckled weakly. "Starving is the least of my problems."

"Are your legs broken? They look broken in two."

This was the first real conversation they had had since the accident. He seemed to be rallying.

"Yes. I think they are both broken and I have a tree in my . . . under my gut." Teg coughed, wincing at the pain.

"Well, that's pretty awful. I guess it hurts real bad."

"It does. It hurts something terrible. How am I still alive? I should be dead by now."

"Maybe the Devil and Jesus are fighting over who has to take you."

"I'm not that bad, little girl."

"You're bad enough."

CHAPTER 42
A BAD GUY'S OUT THERE SOMEWHERE

Dan answered the phone the next morning. My siblings and I had sat up late talking, and we were sleeping in a little. The ringing land line woke me up. I could hear Dan thanking Mom for the pie. They could just chat a minute. I lay there thinking my thoughts, but I was awake. Might as well get up.

I spotted Roxie, asleep on the gas logs in the living room fireplace, as I walked through to the kitchen, tying my robe. Dan was still on the phone.

"You don't say?" . . . "No kidding." . . . "Yes, we watch the news every night." . . . "Okay, I'll tell them. Better yet, here's Penny. I'll let you tell her."

Dan grinned as he handed me the phone. I hadn't even had coffee yet. He carried his to the living room.

"Morning, Mom. What's up?"

"Lord, you need to be up and watching the news.

"Why's that?

I tried to reach the percolator, but the phone cord wasn't quite long enough. I've told Dan we need to replace it. The phone, not my percolator. I loved my coffee pot. But we could sure use a portable phone. Especially right then, when I needed coffee.

"Oh, Lord a mercy. It's just awful. There's a murderer running around loose and he's heading your way."

"Hang on Mom."

I let the cord dangle, retrieved a tall ceramic cup from the cabinet, poured myself some coffee, stirred in sweetener, took the half n half from the fridge and shook it so it would be foamy like a latte, and poured it into my steaming cup. I took a big sip and swallowed. I took a second sip, and then, I picked the receiver back up and held it to my ear.

"Sorry, Mom. What's that you said?"

"There's a MURDERER down there. His name is Teg Duke. Lawsy, it's bad. It's all over the news. Why aren't you watching?"

"Some of us sleep, Mom. Some of us sleep past . . . I looked at the clock on the stove . . . past seven fifteen."

"This man . . . this Teg Duke, he just got out of prison. They said he could be right there in your town."

"Mom are you talking about that guy that killed his parole officer and a nurse a couple of weeks ago?"

"Well, now if you watched the news every once in a while you'd know all the facts. It was the manager of his halfway house. Why do they let folks like that out of prison for anyway? That woman was a hospice nurse taking care of his daddy. And, he killed his daddy, too. Did you hear about that?"

"Yes, Mom. I did. IT WAS OVER A WEEK AGO."

"Well, now they've connected him to that murder of those two teenagers at the motel in Fairplay the other day. Fairplay's between you and Douglasville. Did you know that?"

"I know where Fairplay is, Mom. I've heard about that murder, too . . . those murders, I mean. I didn't hear that they were by the same person."

"That's because you aren't up watching the news! And, that's what the police say! They say it's the same guy. You and Pam and Brett need to stop poking around in the woods. What if he's hiding there?"

I sipped my coffee. My mean streak kicked in. "Well, Mom. What if, instead of here, he got right back on the freeway and headed up to Blue Ridge?"

Silence . . . then, "Tell Brett to get back up here right now."

"Mom, seriously, we'll be careful. The people we're looking for is a little girl and, maybe, a pedophile, kidnapper."

"Well, miss smarty, that's what Teg Duke is."

I looked at my coffee, already needing a refill. "What?"

"He's a child molester. I saw it on the news."

For the second time in two days, I felt that goose bump making chill form across both arms and down my back.

I waited for Dan to leave for his Saturday morning golf date, to tell Pam and Brett what she'd said. Dan had cooked them bacon, eggs and pancakes and they were at the table enjoying their breakfast.

I added, "I mean it really doesn't mean anything. Know what I mean?"

Pam nodded, "Lots of child molesters, rapists, sexual predators out there. Probably hundreds right around you."

"I don't think so." I was indignant.

Brett opened his I Pad and did a child molester search for our town. He showed me a map with lots of colored lit up dots, some just a street away. I was horrified. I had no idea.

"They ARE everywhere. Look." He typed in other small towns so I could compare and he was right. Every town around us had them.

"So, chances are that it may be a normal perv instead of a murdering perv?" There was no comfort at all in that thought.

Pam suggested, "Why don't you call that cute officer Chad I met the other night and discuss it with him."

"Sure. While I'm at it, want me to make you a dinner date at Little Hawaiian, Pam?"

Just to appease my jitters, I did call Chad. He told me that every sexual predator in Carrollton had been checked out and cleared when the little girl disappeared. Despite the fact that the police were sure she had drowned, they did the predator round up as a matter of policy. It was standard protocol with any missing child case.

"So, could it be this Teg Duke that everyone is looking for?"

He was kind, but firm. "First of all, she's dead. Drowned in the river. We'll find her soon, when the river settles back down, and you will stop worrying. And second of all, if it is Teg Duke, she's also dead. I've seen the crime photos of the trail of murders he's left."

"I understand what you're saying."

"She's dead and I'm sure he's long gone. If he's around, which I doubt, we'll get him soon enough. Say 'Hi' to your twin for me. What's her name?"

I winced, because I knew my sister could hear my response, "Pam. The name is Pam. Thanks, Chad." I hung up the phone.

"What? Was he asking about me?" Pam's voice went up to a High C note.

"No. He's making cookies in the kitchen at the station and wants to know what to spray on his pans."

Deflated now, "Oh."

I told Pam and Brett the rest of the conversation. I refuse to encourage Pam's cougarism.

Pam and Brett googled everything they could find out on Teg Duke. I paid no attention as I didn't think he could possibly be connected to the missing Cara.

Brett said, "Look at this picture of him. He's got a lot of tattoos. See these numbers? They mean he's a racist."

Pam looked at him. "How do you know that? Explain."

I don't know why she bothered asking. Our brother always knows weird, random things that no one else seems to know. Brett had called me a few months ago to chat. And then, clear out of the blue, he told me that most folks don't wash their dominant thumb when they wash their hands. We had quite the conversation about it, and now I'm overtly aware of it whenever I wash mine.

Brett said, "I'm not sure about the 14, but the 88 may stand for Adolph Hitler. Eight is the position of H in the alphabet, and white supremacists use it."

Pam was surprised. So was I. "No kidding?"

Brett shrugged. "Well, it could also represent the 88 keys on a piano or the fact that there are 88 constellations in the universe."

I shook my head. My brother is a wonderment of trivial knowledge.

CHAPTER 43
DAY 6

Cara opened the door and poured out her bag of pee and poop. She had perfected the process with her grocery bag. The smell was terrible. But most of the odor came from the front seat.

That Duke man just pees on his own self I gess. I cant help that. It stinks so bad tho. He sits in his own pee. So gross.

Cara had contemplated using the empty peanut butter jar for her toileting, but it served much better as a container to collect rain. The traces of peanut butter helped flavor the water. She knew the rain would stop at some point, so she kept her boot full, too.

As she filled the jar, she looked down at the creek. It was a lot closer to the bottom of the car. Her daddy had told her that the river would rise, and now the creek was doing that, too.

Maybe if the water gets up to the car we can just flote down the river like we are riding in a boat. I could flote it home.

Cara gave Teg some water and then settled back to draw a picture of a boat paddle.

She had used the knife two days before to cut three slits in the back seat upholstery, and at night, she would slip underneath to sleep. A pulled wedge of foam over her lumpy backpack provided a pillow.

CHAPTER 44
LITTLE GIRL LOST

I couldn't think of Cara and Leman without thinking of my own father and what he would do . . . did do . . . if I was lost. My mother, too.

I was ten when we first moved to Georgia. My parents rented a house on Dura Lee Lane, off of Bankhead Highway in Douglasville, while our new house was under construction. Dad would be retiring from the US Air Force soon. Time to settle down. A recruiter, working with young men and women joining the service, his office was in Atlanta about forty-five minutes away.

It was late July and very hot. We had only been in the rental house a week. That morning Brett and Pam were finishing their chores. Mom was home, too, bustling around in the kitchen unpacking boxes of dishes and cookware and arranging them in the cabinets. She wouldn't start working at the hospital until we were all settled and school started at the end of summer.

I had finished my own chores early and left my siblings behind. My sister and I had met Rachel a couple of days before, and were delighted to find out she would be entering seventh grade with us. I was too eager to share my new Tiger Beat magazine with my new friend to wait for Pam. Her driveway was long and winding and, though it opened to our street, the house was actually behind ours, separated by a fence and connected by a private driveway.

I rode my bike up the street right past the entrance to Rachel's driveway and, confused, turned at the top of the road on to busy Bankhead Highway. Even as an adult, I'm teased about being directionally challenged. I pedaled awhile and realized I had made a mistake. When I turned around to make my way back, I couldn't find our street . . . couldn't even remember the name of it.

I didn't know it at the time, but I had pedaled past our road. Everything looked so unfamiliar. At some point a dog ran after me, barking . . . growling. I pedaled faster. Large semi-trucks honked as they passed by me. I entered a zone of pure adrenaline, fear, and anxiety. And, so, I just kept on pedaling.

Pam arrived at Rachel's house an hour later. When she saw I hadn't made it, she dropped her bike and ran home, climbing over the fence, to tell our mother. Mom, with growing panic, drove around looking for me. I can't imagine her fear. Well, actually I can. We once lost Meagan for hours at Disney World. So, I do know that helpless feeling. Mom called Dad in Atlanta. He left for home immediately.

My dad was just sure I would be home before he got there. Cell phones didn't exist in those days so he couldn't check for news as he drove. Traffic was bad, and it took him well over an hour. I was still gone, when he arrived. He and Mom began to search together, driving up and down streets looking. Pam and Brett stayed home in case I returned.

I pedaled past a sign that said, *"Welcome to Lithia Springs."* I knew then that I wasn't in Douglasville anymore. I could go no further and I needed help. I turned into a neighborhood, stopped at the first house on the corner, and got off my bike. My legs were wobbly from exhaustion. I knocked on the front door, and a lady opened it. I was crying and babbling as she brought me inside and gave me a glass of water. I must have made no sense, because she soon put me in her car and took me to Sheriff Earl Lee's office.

The gruff sheriff gave me the third degree about what I was doing on the highway.

"Your parents let you ride your bike on Bankhead Highway?"

I didn't know how to defend my parents or myself, because I didn't fully understand how I'd gotten myself lost.

Sherriff Lee scared me to death. I don't think I ever thought to tell him we'd only lived there for a week and that's why I didn't know. I was embarrassed that I didn't even know my phone number. Finally, getting nowhere, he had an officer drive me around.

Teary eyed, I pointed at things I remembered passing and we were soon back in Douglasville. I had been gone for hours and the sun was beginning to set. We passed my father's car. "Daddy" I squealed. The officer made a U-Turn and flashed his lights to stop them. Mom was in the passenger seat. I could see tears in her eyes.

I remember that hug from my father. It was all encompassing and warm and just what I needed. My mom's, too . . . the dissolving fear . . . no anger at what I'd done . . . only relief. With me in the back seat sobbing, my parents followed the officer to Lithia Springs, to the lady's house, to retrieve my bike. They were shocked at how far I'd gone.

Of course, the story is repeated to this day at family gatherings. Ten years old, I had ridden my bicycle over ten miles by myself to another town, when I only had to go three driveways up from our house to a home I could see from our back porch. And now, as an adult, I still get lost sometimes . . . okay, often. And I don't have my daddy anymore to look for me. But I do have Dan and my friends and thankfully, a GPS.

CHAPTER 45
DAY 7

I dont have any more bread or peenut butter. My tummy is growling like a grizzly bear.

Cara looked at the canned goods and selected a can of corn. She tried to stab it with the big knife, but the blade didn't pierce the can. Instead, her hand slipped down the blade and she gashed three of her fingers. Blood poured from the wounds. She opened the door and held them out in the now drizzling rain. The water stung the wounds badly, and her eyes teared up. But, she was done crying.

No sounds came from the front seat today. Teg was slipping in and out of a coma now. He rarely moaned.

Cara took some upholstery strips she had cut from the car and wrapped them around her fingers. She used the handles from one of the grocery bags to wrap around the fabric, to hold it in place. The cuts weren't too deep and the stinging subsided, but the hunger pangs remained.

Cara's daddy had showed her a trick one time, opening a can of tuna fish on a boat ramp on one of their many camping trips. He had brought a can opener, but wanted to show the trick off. Cara wasn't sure she was strong enough, like her daddy. But, she was hungry and willing to try.

She opened the car door and held the can top against the rocks and began scraping. She scraped until her arm ached and then she would rest a little, before beginning again. About an hour into her mission, she saw juice run out of the can. Cara scraped harder, her excitement growing. The lid fell off, spilling most of the contents into the creek below.

Cara ate the remaining cold corn and drank the juice from the can, savoring the flavors.

You dummy. Next time dont spill the food in the river. The fish have their own food. They dont need mine. I need a fishing pole.

Cara drew a picture of a rod and reel with a colorful rainbow trout hanging from the line. Even if she had one, she wouldn't have used it. No way could she eat raw fish.

To bad cars don't come with micowaves.

After she ate the corn and made her journal entries, Cara lay on the floor board with the door open. The rain had stopped and she enjoyed the fresh clean air. She searched the water below for fish, but the flooding waters were brown and murky. She couldn't see anything.

Cara could hear cars and big trucks rumbling over the highway to the right and above. She would yell as loud as she could, even though no one could hear her. She even thought she saw the edge of a boat go by on the creek below, but her yells were covered up by the roaring flood waters. And, the river was slowly rising.

CHAPTER 46
PLATES

Dan was frying up bacon, and I had my hands deep in dough, making Sunday morning biscuits. Okay that's a lie. I buy them already formed and frozen from Mary B's at Publix. They come in a Ziplock bag. But I WAS putting them on a cookie sheet and cooking them in a hot, preheated oven. Brett and Pam were sitting at the kitchen table drinking coffee when the phone rang.

I asked, "Do one of you mind getting that?"

Pam picked up the receiver from the wall and said, "Hello? Lewis residence . . . Oh, hi. Hang on a second."

She covered the receiver and said, "It's for me." Pam stepped into the garage closing the door over the cord. I guessed she wanted some privacy. It would be hours later that it would occur to me to wonder who would call Pam on our land line.

My siblings and I returned to the river and spent the day looking for something, anything that might be a clue. We couldn't find a thing. Whatever might have been there had been washed away by continuous heavy rains that had fallen intermittently for the last four weeks. But at least it wasn't raining on that Sunday.

Brett spotted a few more Midland water snakes, and Pam and I grew less afraid of them, even stepping over a sleeping snake on one of the paths we followed. But no evidence, no clues were to be found.

We drove back to the house to change. My Widow's Club was meeting that night at Plates in Adamson Square, and the girls had asked me to bring along Brett and Pam, and even Dan if he wanted to come. My husband absolutely refused. He said he'd prefer to eat a sandwich rather than sit around talking to women who might want him offed to make me a legitimate member.

I rolled my eyes at that and kissed Dan goodbye as we headed out the door. I knew full well that my husband was not worried about me or anyone else murdering him. He just wanted some quiet time away from my chatty brother and sister. That, I fully understood. And truth be told, I think he was still a little queasy from eating almost an entire chocolate chip pecan pie.

We were ushered upstairs, as usual, by the hostess at Plates. We tend to get rowdy at these dinners, and so, we were always seated up above, away from civilized guests. Lizzy was bubbling over relaying to Martha, Deborah, Candy, and Kay about our adventure in the woods. I whispered to Brett not to ruin her fun by explaining that the snake wasn't venomous. He chuckled and agreed.

We placed our drink orders and I could see the other ladies were already into their second glasses. Deborah was especially giggly. As designated driver, I would nurse one glass of wine all night, supplementing with iced tea . . . no lemon.

Brett soon had the group entranced with his tales of Julius Squeezer. All of these women had lost their husbands . . . to cancer . . . to heart disease . . . and one to a motorcycle accident. I watched their faces, all joyful, squealing in mock horror as Brett entertained them. I loved these ladies dearly and appreciated that they included me. Although I was certainly sometimes a golf widow, I still had a loving husband, and they didn't. I would never take that for granted. And I hoped to never share their grief.

I ordered the Steak Hibachi . . . my favorite. Brett decided on the Elk Meatloaf, and Pam the Charleston Shrimp and Grits. The food came up from downstairs on a Butler's elevator near our table and was served to us by a lovely young waitress, who often joined in the laughter. The noise was so loud and boisterous that I never heard my cell phone ring. It wasn't until the caller left a message, and I felt the vibration in my pocket, that I took it out and looked. I listened to the message.

"Pam, can you walk out on the balcony with me for a sec?"

"Okay." She looked puzzled.

We stepped outside on the small balcony that looked out over Adamson Square.

"Do me a favor and stand next to the wrought iron railing?"

"Why? Are you going to take my picture?" She leaned her back against the iron and posed with a smile and her arms outstretched. The street lights of the square lit her dark hair and green hazel eyes nicely.

"It's because at the end of this conversation, I intend to push you over the side and splatter your guts on the sidewalk below."

She lowered her arms and stepped forward, her smile gone.

"What did I do?"

"Did you talk to a reporter this morning while I was cooking breakfast? On my phone?"

"I did."

"Did you make an appointment with her in the morning to talk to us?"

"I did."

"Can I ask why? Have we not had enough publicity about the whole decapitation murder and your bronco riding on a bad guy wrapped in a cheap motel bedspread? Seriously? Have you not had enough? Because, I sure have."

"Let me explain."

"I'm waiting. You have about thirty seconds before I shove you over the railing."

"It's been two weeks since Cara disappeared. Nobody's talking to the police. If they know something, they aren't saying. However, it occurred to me that Leman knew who you were from the newspaper articles and reached out to you. Maybe someone knows something and, just maybe, they will talk to us if they know we are helping."

"Why us? Why not the police?"

"I'm telling you it's something I have a feeling about."

"Your intuition?"

"Exactly. Can we go back in now? Or are you really going to murder your own twin sister?"

I stepped to the railing and looked down.

"Nah. Not this time. The Square looks too pretty tonight to mess it up with your guts."

We walked back inside to loud gales of laughter, and I noticed my brother's face was red as a pickled beet. I also noticed that Deborah had scooted her chair awfully close to Brett. Lord, there are cougars everywhere.

Pam sat down and asked, "What did we miss? What's so funny?"

Lizzy threw her head back, holding her stomach. She was laughing hysterically. Martha had her forehead on Candy's shoulder. The both of them snorting and giggling. Kay's mouth was wide open in shock, her hand holding a glass of chardonnay suspended in the air.

"Tell us!" I said. I had to hear the story. My anger at my sister was dissipating, and I needed some good humor myself.

Lizzie gasping for air said, "Tell them, Deborah."

Deborah said, "You tell them, Lizzie. I'm not repeating the story."

Lizzie wiped the tears from her eyes on her napkin and said, "Okay, I'll tell it. Listen to this. I got Deborah on match.com. Remember?

"I do." Oh this is going to be good, I thought.

"So, Deborah goes out with this guy she meets online to a restaurant, and one thing leads to another, and they end up back at her house, IN BED!"

"Okay." Did I really want to know this?

"Anyway, they are having passionate sex and Deborah starts hearing this funny noise." Lizzie was in stiches again and we had to wait for her to gain her composure.

"Lizzie Barganier! Pull yourself together." I was laughing, too.

She tried her best, "The noise was, *Clickety Clack, Clickety Clack, Clickety Clack.*"

All the girls were laughing loudly. Brett was covering his face with his hands, his shoulders shaking.

Deborah tried to look solemn, but couldn't. A small giggle escaped.

Pam and I looked at each other. We had no idea what could be so funny.

"What in the world was it?" asked Pam.

Lizzie snorted, "So then, Deborah asked him if it was his leg making that noise, and he said it was." Lizzie lost it again.

Deborah took over, "So I looked under the covers and realized he had a prosthetic leg. I asked him 'What happened to your leg?' and he said . . ."

She started giggling and took a sip of wine.

"And?" I asked.

"He said, 'Shark Bite'."

Oh, my goodness. We were all laughing so loudly, the restaurant manager had to come upstairs and nicely shoosh us.

CHAPTER 47
DAY 8

There is the cutest chipmunk on the front of the car. He climbed down the rocks all by himself. Hes a very very brave chipmunk. I keep trying to draw him but he wont sit still.

Not even for a minit!! Hes just so cute.

The man isnt talking at all anymore. Hes not drinking any water ether. I think he might die soon. He smells really bad.

The sound of helicopters was overhead. The vibrations shook the car violently. Cara hoped they were looking for her. She had no way to look up and the rattling both unnerved and excited her.

"Please, please, please, find me."

Cara wondered if her daddy was in one of the helicopters. She knew he would be doing everything he could to find her, but it had been a long time. The sounds grew distant and her shoulders sagged. She looked back at the front window. The chipmunk was gone, too.

CHAPTER 48
PAPARAZZI

The reporter from the local paper, Sula Belle Mathis, arrived at my house, sharply at ten. We sat in the living room for the interview. I served her coffee from my percolator, and she commented that her great grandmother used to have one just like it. I ignored Pam's knowing look and smiled when the reporter commented how good the coffee was. Sula Belle had a tape recorder and a note pad, and we got started on the interview.

As usual, we rehashed the Tennessee escapade. We took turns telling Sula Belle about our journey to photograph roadside crosses for Mom. We showed her the collection of pictures on my laptop and allowed her to slide some of them onto a flash drive for her story.

We also told her about our cousin Jacey . . . how we'd ended up in Athens when Mom called to tell us that Jacey had been arrested for cutting off her husband Junebug's head. And we talked about the funny attorney and his funnier secretary. All through the story, Sula Belle would stop us for clarification on one fact or another like, "When did you first suspect Jacey was innocent?" and "What made you think the Harley keychain was significant?" Lots of questions and lots of answers that ended with me conking out a bad guy with a coffee pot and Pam rolling him up in a bedspread and sitting on him like a cowgirl until the police arrived to make the arrest.

Then, the discussion switched to the case of the missing Cara Garrett. I explained about meeting Leman at the Walmart. Sula Belle even listened raptly to my saga about the microwave and the pillowcases. At least she cared about my personal trauma.

Pam told the reporter that she was just sure the little girl was alive and, if anyone else thought the same, they should contact us.

Sula Belle asked, "Why are you so sure? The police . . . everyone else thinks she drowned in the Little Tallapoosa.

Pam said, "We know they do. But I've had these dreams . . ."

I interrupted, "Pam's not a psychic or anything like that. She just has a very strong intuition." I sure don't want the whole town to think my family is nuts, even if it's true.

Then Pam laid a bombshell, "I'm pretty sure that pedophile murderer everyone is looking for has her. That Teg Duke guy."

I was horrified. "Oh Pam. Why would you go there? We know no such thing."

Sula Belle was surprised herself of, course, and scribbled in her notes. She then asked Brett how he was involved. Brett responded, "I pretty much keep my sisters safe from snakes."

Following the interview, we sat for a photo shoot. Brett's bald head kept making a glare, and so this took quite a bit of time.

The article with lots of pictures came out in the Times-Georgian the next day. It was very well written and more truthful than a lot of the stories we had read about ourselves. I just wished Sula Belle had left out the part about Teg Duke. Unknown to us, the story was also picked up by the Associated Press and would be in the Atlanta papers on Wednesday with the headline ***DETECTIVE SISTERS AT IT AGAIN***. Lord.

CHAPTER 49
DAY 9

Cara unwound her makeshift bandage from her hand. The cuts didn't bleed anymore, but the wounds were red and very tender. Still, she left the bandage off as it hindered her drawing and writing.

She began with the rocky crags that surrounded her. She couldn't see the trees, but she knew they were there and drew them in from memory. She didn't include the SUV but sketched as if she were in the river, looking up at the mountains that rose on each side of her.

Cara pulled out her pack of color pencils from the front pouch of her backpack. They were not cheap Dollar Store pencils but an expensive gift from her father, purchased at a real art store. Cara used them sparingly in her artwork, wanting them to last forever. The landscape she was creating was color pencil worthy she decided. She wet the tip of the emerald green pencil with her tongue and began shading the largest tree.

CHAPTER 50
ESCAPADE

My kitchen phone rang while I was making a pot of coffee Wednesday morning. Dan was in the shower, and my siblings were beginning to make stirring noises from their rooms. Roxie was draped over the bottom rung of a kitchen chair, fast asleep. The dowel pressed deep into her stomach in a most uncomfortable way.

I shook my head at my crazy cat and answered the phone, "Hello?"

I didn't recognize the voice. "Is this Ms. Lewis?"

"It is."

"How you doing, ma'am?"

"I'm sparkling. Who is calling, please?"

"I can't tell you my name, ma'am, but I might know something you could use to find that little girl. I found your number in the phone book."

Another reason to disconnect the house phone, I thought.

"Okay. I'm listening."

"It's about that car Teg Duke is driving. See the po po they don't know this. But, Voncille had problems with her tranny in her Honda and she dropped her car off at my place for me to look at it. That's the same day she was killed."

"The po po?"

"Police, cops . . ."

"Gotcha."

"Well now the po po do know that part. They found Voncille's car out in my front lot. I quit working on it when I heared she was dead. Ain't nobody to pay me, now. You feeling me? So they know that's where it is. They just don't know that I loaned her my car til I could get her transmission swapped out. I told 'em she walked to work."

I was indignant. "Why in the world wouldn't you tell the police the truth? That's pretty important."

"Well see, my car ain't registered and there ain't no insurance either. I don't have no proof I bought it. You feeling me? I didn't wanta get in no trouble, so I didn't tell the po po. But if he's got that little girl. Well then that's a whole different problem, ain't it?"

I agreed that it was. "Tell me whatever you can."

"Will you swear on your mama that you won't tell I called? You and your brother and sister . . . you just use this information your own self and find that child. Don't want nothing to happen to that little girl. I gotta little daughter in Alabama my own self. You feeling me?"

I made a solemn promise that I wouldn't tell on him, but I left my mama out of it.

The man, whoever he was, told me the car was a 2012 black SUV Ford Escapade. He even gave me the license and VIN numbers.

As soon as we hung up, I called my favorite po po, Chad, at the Carrollton Police Department and filled him in.

Chad was delighted and furious at the same time. "What an idiot. Whoever the man is that called you, the Atlanta police will know his name, because they've already been to his garage to look at Voncille's Honda. They will know exactly who he is."

"I thought the same thing. He IS an idiot if he thinks we . . . you . . . wouldn't figure it out."

"He's also partly responsible for those Douglas County teenagers at the motel getting killed. He should have been honest when the police talked to him. They could have had an APB out on the Escapade weeks ago. This just makes me furious."

"Yep. That's exactly why I don't feel guilty for breaking the promise I made him." I almost added, "You feeling me?" But, I resisted.

Chad thanked me and hung up to contact the Atlanta and Douglas County investigators.

Pam was pleased as punch when she finally dragged herself to the kitchen and I told her what had happened.

"Aren't you glad you didn't throw me over that wrought iron railing now? Our publicity has already shown results." She poured herself a cup of coffee.

"I suppose so. Here's the half n half."

Brett soon joined us and was amazed that something had happened so quickly. But it wasn't really all that fast. After all, this child had been gone for nearly two weeks. Where was she?

CHAPTER 51
DAY 10

Mr. Duke is awake today. He isnt saying anything. He is just looking at me. I moved to the front seat for a little while to keep a watch on him. He drunk some of the water I gave him, but that is all. He didnt seem intrested in my can of chilly. Cold chilly isnt so bad. I wish it was warm though.

I dont want to draw him. If I ever get out of this car, I dont want to member him. Is that mean? I hope not. I will say Im sorry in my prayers tonight if it is.

I had a dream last night. The lady with the black hair gave me sparkles.

CHAPTER 52
PENPALS AND PENAL PARFAITS

Brett was a tad hung over from our dinner at Plates. So he and Pam got a late start on the river search. They left for the boat ramp around eleven. I had declined to go with them as my PenPal Writer's group was meeting at Eleanor Hoomes' house at noon. I would join my siblings later, but I knew the two of them would send me plenty of text messages to keep me updated. I had to silence my phone so that the constant pings didn't disturb my friends, but I would know from the vibration signal.

Beverly, Cecilia, Donna, Claire, and Sue were already there when I arrived. We assembled in the beautiful dining room with a view of the lake out back. Eleanor had made a ham with a carrot/pea medley and potato salad as good as Mama's. The lunch was served on her fine china with six large silver candlesticks in the middle of the table.

Dessert was a chocolate striped ice cream cake. An enthusiastic discussion followed. We all wanted the recipe and felt like it was in need of a better name than just "ice cream cake." As we talked, we found ourselves leaning to one side or the other of the candlesticks. It was like looking through jail bars. That, and the chocolate stripes on the cake, inspired Claire to call the cake "Penal Parfait." For some reason, Eleanor didn't find that nearly as humorous as we did. That's just too bad, as that is what we will forever call the delicious dessert.

We chatted about all that happened in our lives since we'd met the month prior. Cecilia was worried about the unrest in her home country, Colombia. Eleanor and Wendell were leaving the next day for a trip to the mountains. Donna told us that Curtis was having a huge tree in their front yard carved by an artist with a chainsaw. It was to become two giant bears on a mountain with a cabin on top. We promised to stop by and see it. Beverly was excited about Bob getting a hole in one out at Sunset Hills. I promised to let Dan know. Sue had contracted with a church for a series of plays she was both writing and directing, and we made plans for a group trip to her opening night. Claire had her little granddaughters over for the weekend and shared several cute stories about them. I felt that familiar pang of jealousy shared by the grand-childless.

After lunch, we moved to the living room and the readings began with a new poem by Eleanor. It was a lovely ode to the ending summer. I listened to it as I checked my phone for messages from my siblings.

A text from Pam read, "Lots of people here to help today. I guess most of them know u. They r asking when u are coming."

I replied, "Still tied up. Probably three-ish."

Eleanor's next poem caught my attention. I smiled at the charming, girl empowering, story as she recited it.

A FAIRY TALE
Yesterday I read a fairy tale set in a long ago time and a far away land, about a beautiful princess in peril and the brave hero who rescued her. But— if I had woven the fairy tale, hereafter, the hero would have been in peril, and amid page-turning suspense and laughter, the princess would have rescued him into "Once upon a time" and "Happily ever after."

Beverly was next. She's a stunning statuesque blonde who writes children's educational books. A retired teacher, she really knows what appeals to that market and has published several successful series of adventure books. Apparently, she uses her proceeds to keep QVC on the air with numerous jewelry orders. I'm always amazed at the number of rings and bangles that adorn each arm and finger. I admired them all with each turn of her page. I love me some bling. Beverly was reading an adventure story she had written, that time traveled her characters into fascinating historical events. I was captivated.

The phone in my lap vibrated again. This time it was from Brett, and I discreetly read the message.

"These people are still searching down river. Must be 100 peeps here. I think Pam and I are going to move up stream."

"OK. Just keep me posted where you are."

"Will do. Lizzie is with us and Deborah."

I rolled my eyes and turned my attention back to Beverly.

Claire began with a poem, and as is often found in her writings, it was inspired by one of her grandchildren. I was entranced. I couldn't help but think of Cara as she read from **SOPHIE'S SECRET LIFE**.

This afternoon after the rain,
We sat together in backyard swings
While you confided your secret life –
Mysterious forays into another world
That calls to you as dusk descends.
At five, your life teems with silent acts
Practiced in twilight rendezvous fairy school,
Where you and your sister learn the rap
To shake stars of hope from heavenly realms,
To use imagination to shake the world . . .

Claire continued reading the poem as I peeked at my phone.

Pam texted, "Dan is here helping."

Wow. I was surprised. I knew he had a lot on his plate at work. And, he had a bum knee, to boot. He didn't tell me he was going down to the search site. Refocus! I had missed some of Claire's wonderful poem, but tried to at least hear the end.

I look at golden curls framing your golden face,
And envision you carrying your love into the future.
You will bless the earth and its inhabitants,
If, when you cross the bridge into adulthood,
You take your secret life with you.

Perhaps, I had Pam's sixth sense, after all. I know Pam, Brett, and Dan assumed my painting was a portrait of Cara or maybe one of my daughters, but it wasn't. This poem of Claire's . . . the view from the back of the spritely blonde child . . . the enchanted golden pieces . . . this poem was my painting.

Sue passed out copies of a new play she had written for her church. This was always fun as we were assigned parts to read. I would be playing the part of a Roman soldier. I sat up straight, as my theatre training and Mama had taught me. But the occasional vibration of my phone kept causing me to lose my place. Cecilia would have to nudge me when it was my turn. I was totally destroying the flow of Sue's story and I knew she was probably getting annoyed.

Pam texted, "Dan just discovered there are lots of snakes here. Not sure how long we'll have him. LOL."

Donna had been working for some time on a fascinating story about her father and her resulting childhood experiences. Her father had been involved with gangsters in his day, and her descriptions from that life always had us on the edge of our seats. Each month she read the newest installment, so we were getting the whole story, a little at a time. Donna's stories were my favorites at PenPals. I tried very hard to pay attention.

Then from Dan, "Good Lord. I nearly stepped on a snake! This place is crawling with them. I can't believe you've walking around down here. I'm buying you some boots." His text had a picture of the offending serpent taken from a good distance away. I could tell it was only about eight inches long and the diameter of a pencil, a harmless little garter snake.

It was my turn to read. I opened my manuscript to **Chapter 16, FRIDAY WAS A GOOD DAY FOR A FUNERAL** and began sharing the story of Junebug's funeral. The girls had encouraged me to write about last year's dramatic trip with Pam, and I had done just that. The story turned into a novel that I called BEARING CROSSES. I had numerous query letters out to publishers and hoped one day to see it in print. Each chapter included a picture of one of the many roadside crosses we had photographed.

I could tell they were amused, and I enjoyed the encouraging laughter, mixed with gasping horror as I read.

"The officers released their hold. Then Jacey let out a howl and threw herself forward onto the body, screaming, crying and carrying on like nothing I've ever seen. It was a struggle for the officers to get her off of poor Junebug. And I swear I saw his head roll a bit. Then a lot. All the way to the left side of the coffin toward us. Junebug's head wasn't sewn on at all. It had been perched above his neck and held in place with his shirt collar. My mouth was dry and a bubble formed in my throat choking me. A great upheaval of hellish acid began churning in my stomach. I closed my eyes. I wanted desperately to un-see what I had seen. Not Pam. Pam leaned forward watching."

My phone silently pinged. I tried to ignore it, but I couldn't. I paused in my reading and looked under my manuscript at the screen of my I-Phone. The message was from Brett.

"I found one of her rain boots. Leman's here. He says it's hers."

I must have made some kind of noise because the ladies were all staring at me curiously.

Donna said, "Spill it. What's going on?"

Sue added, "You've been looking at the phone since you got here."

I told them, a little embarrassed, why I had been so distracted throughout their readings. This was very rude of me and I apologized.

"I'm so sorry, ladies. This thing with this little girl is getting to me in the worst way."

Eleanor said, "Nonsense. Don't apologize. I say we postpone this meeting and go help look. You should have told us sooner."

I looked at their lovely outfits and not so sensible shoes . . . at Beverly's turquoise rings and tourmaline bracelets.

"It's muddy down there and the rain is coming again. I don't think . . ."

Beverly waved a jeweled arm and said, "We'll change clothes first. Let's go."

Claire put her hands on her hips. "Rain? Pffff. We won't melt."

Donna stood up and closed her notebook. "If I can get Curtis away from his banjo, I'll bring him along. He's got a machete. Beverly, can Bob help?"

"He'll love it. You know, he's already been on some of the other search teams."

Cecilia Lee clasped her hands in front of her and said, "It would give me great joy to help in this search." I smiled. She has such an elegant manner. She lives three doors up from Eleanor and left to change. The rest of us had to drive to our homes. Relieved but still embarrassed, I apologized again to Eleanor as I walked to the door.

"Stop it. I'll see you at the boat dock in twenty minutes. Sue, I'll find you something to wear." Sue lived too far away to run home quickly, but she really wanted to help. Eleanor hollered down the driveway at Cecilia "I'll pick you up in five minutes, Cecilia." Cecilia waved back in acknowledgment.

And, off we went. These wonderful ladies would help. I'm sure there would be poems and stories inspired by whatever the afternoon would bring. I just hoped it brought something more than a rain boot.

I rushed home to change into jeans and tennis shoes. The rain would begin again soon, so I took the biggest umbrella from the hook in the garage. A smaller one was lying on the concrete floor. I didn't bother picking it up, as I wanted to hurry, so I just stepped over it. As I did, a paw reached out and snagged my ankle with sharp claws digging deep, hitting bone.

"Dang it, Roxie!" I did a dance rubbing at the bloody spots beading up on my sock. My evil cat went back to sleep inside the umbrella.

Brett had found Cara's boot. I was intrigued and a little saddened. Despite Pam's dreams, this didn't sound like a girl who had survived a drowning or a murdering pedophile. I was losing hope that we would find her alive.

CHAPTER 53
DAY 11

Teg dreamed deeply, the pain wasn't so bad anymore. He was able to sleep for days at a time, as if he'd had large shots of morphine . . . floating on a cloud. He would wake for a few minutes and then drift back off. He was at peace most of the time, as long as he didn't move and jiggle the tree branch stuck in his groin. His broken legs had no feeling in them now, so they didn't matter. Sleep was a blessed thing.

Teg dreamed about prison fights and prison food. He dreamed about Jimmy and his peanut butter eyelids. He dreamed about a classmate, Katie from third grade. And he dreamed about home, about his daddy and his mama.

When Teg was a little kid, he had a mama. Her name was Millie. She had long blond hair that hung down her back in cascades of curly ringlets. He could remember her in a hazy sort of way. Folks always said she looked very young, like a kid. This fact was enhanced by a pink ribbon she always wore on the back of her head. The ribbon was as long as her hair and would get caught up and intertwine with her curls.

When the sun was bright, Millie's hair sparkled. He loved that. She used to call him Timmy, he remembered, but over time, she had nicknamed him Teg. He played on the floor with his mama during the times he didn't have school, toys spread across the rug. They made castles with blocks and read books together. She helped him build forts out of the sofa cushions and battled with him with flying Cheetos. She told Teg they would grow up together.

Millie was only fourteen when she married Angus. Millie's parents first met Angus at a bar they all frequented. The couple wanted to make a clean start in California to avoid fraud charges they faced in Georgia. So, they struck a deal with Angus. He needed a wife and they needed a reliable car. He traded his 1980 Chevette with a full tank of gas for a forged marriage license and their daughter. Millie conceived Teg on her wedding night.

She cautioned her son that his father was older, more than thirty, and that he didn't remember his childhood like she did. So, Teg would help her right the house before Angus came home. And when he did, the playing stopped. Teg understood the rules.

His daddy was always mean. He would come home and eat dinner at the kitchen table, ignoring Teg for the most part. His mama would hardly ever sit at the table with them. She stood at the counter the whole time, nibbling from a plate on the stove, ready to get her husband the salt or fill his glass with beer. Whatever he needed, he barked, and she jumped.

Sometimes Angus would punish Teg. This usually happened after dinner. If he detected insolence in the boy's eyes, or if Teg took too long on a chore, the belt would come off. Millie would step in and beg her husband to stop. The beatings would turn to her, and Teg would run and hide in his closet, until Angus tired of it all and collapsed in his recliner.

Most evenings, beatings or not, Angus would sit in the recliner, foot rest up, and watch TV until he fell asleep. Or, on other days, he would grab Millie by the arm and drag her into the bedroom, slamming the door shut. On those occasions, Teg would sit outside their door and listen. He could hear loud grunts and moans, and he knew that his daddy was hurting his mama. There was nothing he could do about it. If Millie cried out, Teg would cover his ears and squeeze his eyes shut, but he would remain sitting with his back against the door.

Later, his mama would come out of the bedroom. Her eyes would be tear stained as she straightened her house dress and walked to the kitchen to clean up the dishes. Teg would often stand beside her and help . . . not speaking . . . just being.

Sometimes, Teg would cry or tremble following these events, and his mama would soothe him by singing country songs. She would dry his eyes on a dish towel and sing Loretta Lynn or Dolly Parton, even Patsy Cline, while she scrubbed pots and pans at the sink. Her voice was beautiful. She sang quietly, almost a whisper, so as not to wake her husband.

One night, Teg was in bed close to falling asleep. It had been a great evening. He had turned six that day, and his mama had baked him a chocolate cake with six real wax candles to blow out. His daddy hadn't come home by dinner time, so Millie had served them both macaroni and cheese and hamburger steak with catsup. And she'd actually sat at the table and dined with her birthday boy. Millie had put on a pretty dress and some lipstick for the occasion.

After they cleaned up the kitchen, and Angus was still not home, they celebrated by eating a second slice of the cake. Then Teg took his bath and brushed his teeth, ready for bed. Millie tucked him in, her golden curls falling across his face as she kissed his cheek and told him, "Nighty night Sweety Pie . . . Six years old! . . . You're nearly a man."

Teg smiled and threw his arms around his mother's neck.

"Thank you, Mama. I loved my cake."

Teg turned to his side, snuggling under the warm blanket, as his mother closed his door. He was drifting off when he saw his daddy's truck lights through the window. A few minutes later, he heard his daddy come in the door. Angus was loud, demanding his dinner and a beer. Teg could hear muffled voices and now and then. And when Angus yelled, he could make out his father's words.

"It don't matter none if I'm late, woman. You still have to have my dinner hot, damn it."

More muffled voices.

"Why is this cake half ate? . . . I don't give a damn whose birthday it is."

Loud thuds and smacks and the little boy knew his mama was getting a beating. His parents' battle moved into the hallway. Teg curled into a ball under his covers. This time, he didn't cover his ears.

"Who you so dressed up for? And what's that shit on your face? You got a boyfriend now? You feed'n him my food?"

Teg heard fabric ripping and his mama's scream. Her scream was cut short. He could still hear her, though. They were right outside his room and the banging rattled the door frame. Teg thought his mama sounded like he had once when he swallowed a Tater Tot without chewing it first. His mother had smacked him on the back until he coughed it out.

The choking sounds dwindled and for several minutes there was silence. Then Teg heard the sound of something being drug down the hallway. Whatever it was thudded into his door and continued moving. The little boy pulled his blanket over his head, his body shaking. A few minutes later, he heard Angus' truck door slam shut. Teg sat up in bed and looked out the window. He watched his daddy's lights as he drove out of the driveway.

Teg tiptoed out into the hallway to find his mama. She wasn't in the living room or the kitchen. The bathroom was dark. Teg looked in her bedroom. Oddly, the bedspread was off the bed and gone. So was his mama. He was home alone. Scared, he crawled back in his bed and tried his best to stay awake. He wanted to hear his mother's voice. Eventually, he fell asleep.

The next morning, Angus told his son that his whore of a mama had run off with a boyfriend and she wouldn't be back no more. It was just the two of them now. Every day, for months, after school, Teg would run from room to room to see if his mother had come home. She never did.

Teg dreamed of this. He dreamed of chocolate cake and country music. He dreamed of a curling pink ribbon. And he dreamed of his mother's golden hair.

CHAPTER 54
THE BOOT

I drove past the first boat dock and could see hundreds of searchers on both sides of the river. They stretched downstream for half a mile, combing through the tall weeds and out into the surrounding woods. I reached the second boat dock and found only a few cars. Lizzie was talking to Brett, Pam, and Dan. Deborah had left after the first snake sighting. My brother was soaking wet with a blanket wrapped around him.

Most of my writers group pulled in a minute later with Eleanor's car leading the way. Bob and Beverly were already there, just getting out of their car. As promised, Donna had brought along Curtis. He's a big man who looked even bigger with the machete in his hand.

Lizzie had also called in the Widow's Club and Blue Heron ladies along with Mike and Doug from the Tuesday morning gentleman's pottery group. They all knew that parking was limited and had met at the studio and all ridden over together in four cars.

My friends were quickly given an assignment by one of the organizers of the search grid, and off they went. I thought they would be their normal chatty selves, but they looked grim and purposeful. Claire had tears in her eyes already. This was not a fun search, and they knew it.

As I walked toward my husband, I spotted Leman chatting with Officer Chad. The boot was now held by Chad in a clear evidence bag. It would soon be taken to the station.

"How did you find it?" I asked Brett as I kissed Dan on the cheek.

"Dan gets part of the credit. See those boulders out there?"

I looked at the river at where he pointed to. I hadn't seen them before during our searches.

Brett said, "Those big rocks were underwater when we were here earlier. But the river has gone down some now. Dan asked me if they were close enough together to walk on. So I thought, why not. And I did. We did. Dan walked out there, too."

"It's a wonder you didn't both fall in and drown. Looks like you came close."

Brett continued, "We were standing out there in the middle of the river, near where the boat ramp ends, and we noticed how clear the water was becoming. Remember how brown it was after the rain?"

I nodded.

Dan said, "The water is still pretty deep and the current is strong. I'd say it's five feet or so, but you can see to the bottom."

Brett added, "We were really looking at where all the other searchers were. You could see them way down there at the other dock and beyond. Then I looked down, right where I was standing. At first, I thought it was tropical fish. Lots of color swirling around. But, tropical fish don't live in rivers."

I turned to Dan as he said, "Brett hollered for me to join him on his boulder. It was barely big enough for both of us. But I could see what he was looking at. I had no idea what it was. Next thing I know, your brother hands me his shoes and jumps into the river. Straight down."

"That boot was caught good. Took some pulling to get it out, but I got it."

Dan grimaced and rubbed his lower back, "Yeah well, it took some pulling for me to get you out, too."

I noticed then that Dan's shirt and pants were damp. He pulled my brother out of the water! I hoped he hadn't thrown his back out at the same time. I've already been through major spine surgery with him for a ruptured disc. It had been ten years, but still!

"That is awesome. But, both of you need to go home and change before you get pneumonia. We'll take it from here. Go home and rest and drink something hot."

Brett pointed out some areas of interest. Following his suggestions, our group spread out in a grid, looking closely at the ground and in the river for anything else we might find.

Dan drove Brett to the house to change. Thirty minutes later, much to my dismay, they were back ready to go at it again. By then, we were a football field away from the boat dock, steadily making progress, but finding nothing. I was on the grid between Beverly and Bob to my left and Sue and Eleanor to my right. Dan caught up with me.

"What are you doing here, crazy man? I thought you were going to go home and rest. You are limping. You need to get that knee elevated. It's going to rain soon."

He said, "I'm fine. Did you know Roxie is asleep inside of an umbrella in the garage?"

"I do. She attacked me from there. She came at me like a crazy, wicked Mary Poppins." I showed him my ankle.

"Hmmm. It never does that to me. Wonder why?"

I didn't answer him for a long while as we combed through briars and weeds until dusk looking for signs of a little lost girl. The rain began falling as we hurried to the cars.

I said, "Sometimes evil is just evil. There's no explaining it."

Dan didn't know if I was talking about our cat or the search for Cara Garrett. I wasn't sure myself.

CHAPTER 55
DAY 12

Sometimes I move to the front seat. I'm not scared of Mr Duke anymore. Hes real bad sick and I dont no if he can get any better. He sleeps most of the time and sometimes he says stuff in his sleep. Last night he talked about Katie. He said, Katie your real pretty. Can I sit next to you? And I think he said slithering. I couldn't tell real good what it was.

I wonder if Katie is his wife. Who would marry such a mean man? I sure wouldnt that's for sure. When I get married I'm going to find someone nice like my Daddy or my Karate teacher, Mr. Chi.

Im still working on my color pencil art on the last page. Im running out of pages. It started out being these rocks that have us stuck and some trees. But funny thing when I turned it. It looks like a girl! Im going to change the river to a pink ribbon in her hair if my eraser dont tear the paper like it did yesterday on the one I drew of the chipmunk.

My chipmunk came back this morning. I think hes the same one. I named him Chip. I know thats not ariginal but thats what I call him. He climes on these rocks. Hes real cute. I put some tomato sause from the can on the rocks to see if he will eat it. Maybe if I stay in the front for a while he wont be scared. Eating tomato sause is gross but I don't have much cans left. I found some peenut butter in the jar lid, though. Just a little bit but it was so good.

Mr. Duke keeps whispering that same thing. I think hes saying Slytherin. That makes sense to me a whole bunch. Cause if he was at Hogwarts then Harry Potter would make him be at Slytherin with all the evil people.

CHAPTER 56
CLICKER

Dan's knee was so swollen that he had no choice but to stay home and ice it down. He was in the bed with his leg propped on a pillow, an ice pack underneath. I brought in a tea tray full of snacks including his favorite, a hot roast beef sandwich. He was in his happy place, watching a golf tournament.

I sat down next to him on the bed. "You going to be okay while we're gone."

"Yep. I wish you would wait until I could go with you."

"Why? We'll try to stay out of trouble."

"Whatever happens to you, happens to me, too, you know. You're not in this alone."

How sweet. I leaned over to kiss him and he pulled me closer.

My annoying sister banged on the bedroom door, interrupting the moment.

"Later," he said with a wink.

Pam, Brett, and I drove over to Lizzie's and picked her up. As we passed Lake Carroll, I was surprised at how much it had flooded. The rain from the night before had been torrential. I had never seen our lake like this. The water now covered parts of Lakeshore Park, and the spillway looked like Niagara Falls. This didn't bode well for the river levels.

Brett was not surprised. "The ground has got to be saturated from all the rain this past month. It has nowhere to go, but to flood."

I pulled into Lizzie's driveway. Her little dogs, Max and Minnie, were barking and trying their best to eat my tires. I honked my horn at the same time Dan called.

"Did you change the sheets on our bed?"

"I did. Why?"

"I can't find the clicker."

"The clicker?" I knew exactly what he meant. But, I acted like I didn't. Thirty-two years of marriage and living in the South with me, and my Pittsburg-born husband still didn't know the proper names for stuff. He calls rubber bands "gum bands," for Pete's sake. Worse, he calls Coke, "soda."

"The clicker . . . the remote control." He sounded really annoyed.

"We have two remote controls in the bedroom. Surely you can find one of them. Look under the bed or the blankets."

"Know what I think? I think you washed them in the washing machine when you washed the sheets?"

"I did no such thing."

"You've done it before."

"Umm. No. I have not."

"Well, you washed something before that wasn't clothing. I remember."

"I've washed tissue that was in your pockets and it shredded all over the washing machine. But, I've never, ever washed a remote control."

"See! That's my point. You don't look."

"Was the remote in your pocket? If it was, then I'll admit the possibility. However, please note that, when I wash the sheets, I don't wash your pants with them. We have king size sheets and they get washed alone. Speaking of which, I think we need new ones . . . and a comforter . . . and a duvet."

"What in the world is a duvet?"

"It's a thing you put on your bed that the remote control sits on, so it never gets lost."

"Well, I'm all for that then. You know, I noticed Roxie slept in our room all day yesterday."

"You think the cat hid our remotes?"

"Well, it might have eaten them."

I giggled. "I think you are on to something there, Dan."

"Come home and push her paw and see if you get *Forensic Files*."

I giggled harder. "Yeah. I'll do that."

He added, "Pull her tail and I bet we get *Seinfeld*."

Lizzie had crated her dogs in the house and climbed into the back seat next to Pam. I had to share this conversation with her and my siblings.

"Dan says he thinks Roxie ate our missing remote controls. Two of them! This is impossible because a) They are about 10 inches long and b) She's a picky eater. But, Dan wants me to come home and push her paw and see if *Forensic Files* comes on. And, he wants me to yank her tail and see if it switches to *Seinfeld*. I think, since he can't change the TV, he just wants to see me get scratched."

Dan interrupted my narration, "Never mind. I found it."

"The cat?"

"No. The clicker. It was on YOUR side of the bed."

I congratulated him with love and we drove on to the river.

CHAPTER 54
DAY 13

Mr. Duke is not saying Slytherin. I was wrong. I think its shimmering. Or shimmery. He must be seeing angels. Nooo that cant be can it? Does it shimmer in Hell? I dont no. I'm only in first grade. I dont want to ever no that.

Shimmery. That's what hes saying. Im pretty sure now.

Cara dug through her backpack and removed a broken yellow pencil that had snapped on the rocks earlier that morning. She had tried to use her left hand to scrape the sides of the pencil on the rocks to create a wide shading edge. Her right hand hurt too much for this job, and she thought she could manage with the left hand. But the pencil had snapped at the point. She hadn't repaired it yet with her little plastic sharpener from her color set, so it had jagged wooden bits where the lead should be.

Cara used the rough wood edges of the pencil as a tool to scrape the metallic gold seals off of the two cans of chili she had already eaten. She did this carefully, scratching around the edges of the gold star seals until she was able to lift them from the can. This took a good while and required several breaks because her hand was very sore, and because she didn't want to damage the paper. When she had both of them successfully removed, she licked the backs of the seals and adhered them to her drawing. The gold pieces sat neatly on the pink ribbon that curled through the blond hair of the girl. Studying the picture up close, Cara wanted more. She needed more. She didn't know why. But it was important. The lady in her dream had told her so. She began searching through the pockets of the seats and in the back cargo area of the hatch.

The little girl looked up from her work as Teg stirred in the front seat. He was dreaming.

Teg dreamed of blood . . . sticky warm blood . . . cupped in his hand . . . dripping from his fingers . . . crusting up under his fingernails. Not a nightmare . . . he liked the feel of it. It eased him.

CHAPTER 57
VENOM

As we feared, the river was overflowing its banks. The water covered the picnic spot and beyond. A few searchers were there but not many. Water was about three inches deep in the parking lot, and we had pulled over on the highway.

Brett suggested we drive up to Tallapoosa and look there. I didn't see the point, but pulled away, back onto the highway headed west. The river was high there, too, but didn't seem to be flooding. So, we got out and looked around.

Lizzie's phone pinged with a new match.com connection.

She showed me her phone. *"Hey there, girl. Let's meet up and eat some spaghetti."*

"Just like Lady and The Tramp," I said.

"You think he wants to slurp a noodle with me?"

"Ew...Gross. Delete him."

She did, and we walked together looking for whatever. We had no idea what we were searching for here. The river was beautiful though, and it was a nice walk . . . muddy, but nice.

Pam and Brett were about fifty feet to our left, close to the river's edge. I could hear Brett chatting about some insignificant fact like he always does.

"Pam, did you know that vampire bats are most likely to bite you on the big toe . . . that is if you are sleeping in a tent and . . ."

Pam said, "Brett, come look. This water snake is bigger than the other ones we've seen."

I saw her bend over to look at it up close. I wanted to see it, too, since there was nothing else to look at. Lizzie followed behind me, clinging to my shoulders. We had finally told her the truth about the snakes, but she was still unnerved by them.

Brett said calmly and quietly, "Don't move. That's a water moccasin."

Bent over, Pam's face was about two feet from the snake. It was curled on a rock, looking up at her. Its tongue flickered.

Brett walked over to a tree and, using his pocket knife, he cut a long branch.

Pam wasn't saying a word, and she remained frozen, her hands on her knees. I could see beads of sweat forming on her forehead. "Dear sweet Jesus sitting on a floating cloud with choirs of Heavenly angels at your hair washed feet," I prayed. "Don't let her drip any sweat on the snake directly below her." And I prayed she would not move a muscle. I could hear her breathing, but it seemed backwards, like she was sucking in air.

Brett tiptoed as quietly as he could on the crunchy fallen leaves to Pam and the snake's right side. The snake pulled its head back and up and opened its mouth. I could see a mass of white tissue and curving fangs. It began bobbing, the head moving further back.

Behind me, Lizzie was making an odd gurgling noise. I tried to shush her, but nothing came out of my mouth.

I was just starting a new prayer, "Dear Angel Gabriel with a golden flute" . . . As the snake struck, Brett whipped it into the air with his branch. The moccasin flew up and over, into the river, where it disappeared from sight. Pam collapsed on the ground, trembling. I'd never seen her that scared.

In a strangled voice she managed to say, "I thought you said there weren't any water moccasins in Georgia."

"No. I said they were rare. This rain has probably brought them to land."

Brett was ready to continue our search, but we three women were done for the day. This was not a sexist issue for us, nor a lack of bravery. Nope, it was pure common sense. We drove back to Carrollton and had a nice, safe, nonvenomous lunch at Little Hawaiian. Pam didn't eat very much. She did have a second glass of wine, though.

Been here 14 days. Theres not much cans left in the bags. I don't know what to do if Daddy doesn't come get me soon. The lady with the black hair visited my dream again. Shes an artist like me. She said I needed more sparkles. I told her I was trying real hard. But I dont feel so good. She said to keep looking. So I will.

While Cara made tick marks on her sketchpad to count the days, Teg dreamed of Katie. He reached out to touch her hair and then jerked his hand back. They were in third grade and Ms. Caponi had put him in the desk right behind the golden haired little girl.

On the playground, Teg sat by himself on a rock. He rarely interacted with the other children. He preferred to sit alone and watch. And, on those days when his bottom hurt, and he couldn't sit on the rock, he would lean against the big elm tree that shaded the playground. Either way, he watched.

Ms. Caponi had noticed the purplish marks on the little boy. She didn't tell anyone. Instead, she would rub her own bruised arms and wonder sadly if the world would ever get any better for anyone. She avoided calling on Teg in class because the other children picked on him, and she thought it better if she didn't encourage their attention.

Boys in the class would hold their noses as they passed Teg's desk. They said he smelled bad. She had noticed that he wasn't the cleanest child herself, but the reactions of the boys were exaggerated and mean. She would tell them to stop and, if she had to, she might write a note to their parents.

The girls didn't pick on Teg, They didn't pay attention to him, either. It was as if he were invisible. They walked past him without speaking or looking at him. He didn't mind.

Some of the girls would bring valentine cards or birthday party invitations and hand them out to all the other children, except for

Teg. A few girls put invite cards on his desk because their mother's made them. Teg knew he wasn't really welcome, and he never asked his daddy to go. The few valentine cards he got, he tucked into his notebook to read later. He stored them in a box under his bed. One of these was from Katie. It smelled like perfume. He kept that one under his pillow.

One day, Ms. Caponi had her back to the class. She was writing spelling words on the chalkboard for the children to copy. One of the words was "shimmery."

Shimmery . . . Shimmery . . . Shimmery. Teg loved that word. He looked at Katie's golden hair and mumbled, "shimmery." *She needs a ribbon*, he thought. He reached his hand up and, this time, he touched her hair.

Katie spun around in her chair and glared at Teg. "Don't you DARE touch me!" The whole class laughed, and Ms. Caponi was looking at him with her forehead all wrinkled up.

"Teg. Please keep your hands to yourself."

Laughter erupted across the room. Some boy yelled, "Ooo Katie's got Teg ticks now. She's gonna smell like butthole." More laughter.

Indignant, Katie said, "No I don't. I sprayed cootie juice on a valentine card and gave it to him last month. It protects me."

The children were howling now. They all knew what cootie juice was. The girls had invented it with cheap perfume.

Ms. Caponi pounded her hand on the desk. "That is enough! Everyone be quiet and copy down these words."

Teg was humiliated. He sank low in his desk. He couldn't copy any more words. Instead, he just wrote "shimmery" all over his page. The giggling of his classmates eventually calmed, and Ms. Caponi continued with her lesson.

CHAPTER 59
SNAKE ATTACKS CONTINUE

Cara had been missing for two weeks, now. Hopes of finding her alive grew dimmer and dimmer. I seemed to be the only person who thought so. Not true. I was pretty sure Dan felt the same way. I got out of bed and went to find my husband.

I heard his scream from the hallway and ran to the living room. Dan was beating something long and slithery with a golf club. I flipped on the light.

Apparently, when I let Roxie out the night before, the sash from my black robe had got caught in the French doors that lead out to the screen porch. I had gone to bed unaware that it was missing. Dan, with our story about the water moccasin fresh on his mind, had come upon my sash. In the dim morning light, it looked like a huge snake crawling through the door.

My husband and I collapsed on the loveseat in laughter. My brother and sister slept through the whole drama.

After we had composed ourselves, we went to the kitchen and made coffee. I pulled a coffee cake from the freezer to heat him up a piece with some warm butter. My new microwave was so spacious, I was able to slide in some for me, too. We sat at the table together and watched the sun come up.

Dan said, "I hope you aren't in for a huge disappointment."

"I know how to handle disappointment."

He looked at me over his cup. "Yeah, well. You still talk about that TV show from when you were a kid. About the Wonder Bread."

I nodded. I've told him the story several times. When Pam and I were in first grade at Ooltewah Elementary School in Chattanooga, our Brownie Troop got to go on the *Bob Brandy Show*. Bob Brandy, his wife Ingrid, and his pony, Rebel, were local celebrities, and their show featured Popeye cartoons. It came on right before *The Little Rascals*.

We sat in bleachers, all of us wearing our Brownie uniforms, giddy with excitement. Bob Brandy, wearing his cowboy hat and outfit, came out to meet us before the show and to warm us up a bit. He told us that sometime during the show, he would be asking us a very special question. Whoever came closest to the correct answer would win a prize.

He said, "Let's practice. Shall we? How many windows are at Rock City?" I sat up straight. Our family had just been there, and I closed my eyes, picturing those windows.

Bob went around the bleachers asking various girls. Their answers were just plain ridiculous. "A thousand! . . . ten thousand . . . A million!" Finally, he came to me. Now I knew it was either six or seven, but I wasn't exactly sure. So, I guessed seven.

Bob nodded his head. "Now, girls, that is closer to the answer I'm looking for."

Now, he hadn't said I was correct, just that my answer was closer. Aha! I thought. I bet it's six.

So during the show, when Bob Brandy asked, "How many windows are at Rock City?" every single girl answered my first answer, "seven." I was the only one who said "six." Every single girl won a package of Wonder Bread hot dog buns except for me. I was mortified and cried all the way home. Pam's offer to share her buns with me did not help one single bit, either.

I've always hated disappointment and failure.

I looked at Dan. "It's not the same thing," I said. "I am not expecting to find her. And, I'm certainly not expecting her to be alive. Whatever happens, I will handle it."

Dan shook his head as he took a bite of my streusel coffee cake. He was skeptical, and I really couldn't blame him. He knows how I dwell on things when they don't work out like I want them to.

The heavy rain came a few minutes later, accompanied all day by thunder and lightning. By evening, our little town had measured four inches. Flooding was reported on special news reports and on our storm radio. No one would be out searching this day. Except Leman. Leman was always searching.

CHAPTER 60
DAY 15

Teg woke from a dream. Cara was wetting his lips with a wet piece of car upholstery. He coughed painfully and drifted back off.

He dont drink water anymore and hes stopped shaking. It rained real real hard today. The river is touching the car now. I can reach down and put my fingers in it. Mr. Duke talks in his sleep some. I dont understand any of it.

Ms. Caponi announced the end of the school "Jump Rope for Heart Campaign." On Friday, she told them, the children would jump rope in the gymnasium for all of the contributors who had given them money. She asked Katie to go around the room and gather up their envelopes. Katie did this proudly, passing by Teg's desk without holding her hand out. She knew, rightly so, that he would not have an envelope. All of the other children did, though. Some envelopes were thicker than others. Some contained just change, and others a combination of bills and change.

Because Ms. Caponi was the Third Grade Jump Rope Chair, she sent Katie to the other classrooms on the hallway to collect their envelopes, too. Katie was pleased and honored to be asked. Carrying a stack of large manila envelopes, she proudly walked out the door. The class that collected the most money would have an ice cream party the following week.

Ms. Caponi asked the rest of the class to get out their reading books. "Turn to page 88," she said. Teg didn't like being there when the desk in front of him was empty. He couldn't hide behind the golden hair. And so he placed his reading book upright on top of his desk, but he didn't open it. Instead, he wrote "88" on his arm with his pencil, digging the lead deep into the skin. It felt good. He dug harder, repeating the pattern over and over, up and down his arm, on the bare skin and through his sleeve. His arm "shimmered" while the rest of the children read quietly.

Ms. Caponi looked over the top of her glasses at her students. They were being very good today. The story they were reading was called "Hoist The Sails," a story they should all just love. It was full of adventure on the high seas. Ms. Caponi was pleased to see that the class was indeed enjoying the story. Then her eyes fell on Teg.

The boy was not reading. His book was closed and standing on its edge. Ms. Caponi quietly stood up and walked over to his desk. Hiding behind the book, he was digging in his arm with a pencil. She could see rivulets of blood on his arm and sleeve.

"Stop right now, young man."

Teg did not respond. Instead, he dug harder making circular eight patterns repetitively up and down the length of his arm. She pulled the pencil from his hand. Teg looked at her. His eyes were deeply dark, unfathomable.

Ms. Caponi whispered, "Why, Teg?"

"I'm shimmery," was his short reply.

Ms. Caponi had mastered the art of speaking low but firm. "Go to the bathroom and clean yourself up." In twenty years of teaching, Ms. Caponi had never seen or heard anything like that before. A few students looked up from their books when they heard her, surprised at the blood dripping from Teg's arm. Most continued reading unaware of the drama a few desks away. Why the boy would hurt himself like that was a mystery to the teacher. She would have to talk to the school counselor later for advice.

Teg walked out of the room and down the hall to the boys' restroom. He wet a handful of paper towels in the sink and massaged his arm, staring in the mirror at his face. His arm was numb and didn't hurt at all.

He heard laughter outside the door. "Thank you, Mr. Grantham. I'll be happy to tell that to Ms. Caponi. She's just sure our class will win the ice cream party. Every student participated this year. Thank you, sir." More laughter.

Teg cracked the door open an inch and peered out. He could see that Mr. Grantham had returned to his classroom. He could see the teacher's back through the slender glass window on the door. Katie stood there in the hallway alone . . . inches from him . . .

shuffling her big yellow envelopes . . . getting them in order. She was engrossed in her task and hadn't seen him.

Teg opened the door wide and grabbed Katie by the arm and pulled her into the boy's room. The door swung shut. He couldn't lock it, but no matter. Startled, Katie let out a small yelp and dropped the envelopes on the restroom floor.

Teg pushed her against the door hard, stunning the little girl. He stared into her wide eyes, clamped his hand over her mouth, and pulled her to the floor on top of the manila envelopes. He fell with her, his body prone on top of hers. With her mouth covered, and her eyes wide with horror, Katie tried to struggle. Teg, much bigger, held her in place with his weight. He began moving up and down. His clothing rubbing on hers. His groin rubbing on her private parts through her jeans.

On the wall behind Katie, protruded a white springy door stop. Her head hit the door stop with the first thrust knocking it off the wall. The door stop bounced off of its anchor across the floor and rolled under the sink. Each following thrust slammed her head into what was left of the small metal anchor. The metal dug deep into her head. Blood spurted through her hair and down her scalp.

Right hand over Katie's mouth, Teg used his left hand to caress and yank at her hair. He could feel the blood pooling wet between his fingers. It felt so good. Better than his growing erection. She kept trying to scream, and Teg pressed her mouth harder, cutting her lips against her teeth. Katie tasted blood. With ecstatic groans, Teg continued the rhythm of his thrusts.

A girl tried to enter the bathroom. Teg was vaguely aware of her. He didn't care. The girl could open the door just far enough to see the bodies blocking the way. With a cry, she ran across to the closest classroom and banged on the door. Then, Teg heard Mr. Grantham's voice yelling. The teacher shoved the door hard enough to push Teg aside, and the boy rolled onto the cold tile floor. Katie was crying . . . then screaming . . . as other teachers came into the bathroom. He was standing now. The teacher had jerked him up to his feet. Mr. Grantham was still yelling, shaking him by the arm. Teg smiled.

The lady teachers calmed and shushed Katie, and then led the girl from the restroom. They wouldn't want the other students to hear her screams. They shielded her, too, so others wouldn't see the blood on her teeth, dripping down her pretty face, and in her hair. They walked her quickly to the counselor's office and called her mother.

Teg was taken to the principal's office and told to sit on a bench. Angus was called. There were several meetings that Teg wasn't a part of, and then, a man came and took him to Juvie for the night. His daddy never looked at him or spoke to him. The next day, Teg was taken to a courtroom and people talked about him, but not to him. He wasn't sure if Angus was there. He never turned to look. No one ever asked him anything. They just took him back to the Juvie and he stayed there for weeks.

Eventually, he talked to a counselor and a doctor, and they sent him to a residential treatment place west of Atlanta. Teg lived there with all boys, attending classes for two years, going to counseling, and group sessions. Those two years at the treatment house were Teg's best. For the first time in his life, he made some friends. He met boys there, just like him. Before returning home to Angus, he learned things from the other boys. They taught him how to unlock a car door without a key. They told him tricks for getting girls to date him even if they didn't want to. They taught him about drugs, too, but that was of no interest to Teg.

Teg and his friends spent a lot of time in the gym and in the weight room. They beefed up . . . developed muscles. Teg's chest broadened and he began to fill out . . . grew tall. His calves rippled as he ran for miles around the track. No one wanted to fight him. He was growing into a big man. And, there was something about his eyes . . . something terrible. Even his friends saw it. The boys who hung out with him, remained wary, but stayed close. They were afraid not to.

Juvie Hall and the residential home would become a revolving door for Teg until he turned eighteen. Most of his crimes were for petty shoplifting until he reached his teenage years. When he turned fourteen, he stole Angus' car a couple of times and beat up a neighborhood boy for no reason. A counselor told the judge that it was her opinion that Teg liked the safe environment of residential treatment and acted out on purpose. She was right. He liked his friends, he liked the kind attendants and teachers, and he liked the structure. Mostly, he liked being away from his father.

As he grew older and bigger, Angus left him alone. The beatings stopped. He saw his daddy's stare when he had his shirt off . . . his muscles bulging. At times, he thought Angus was scared of him. They would go days without speaking, even as they ate dinner at the same table. He hated being home. There was nothing for him there. Yes, he liked living in the residential treatment center and thrived there. He wouldn't feel the same about prison a few years later.

CHAPTER 61
TRAPPED WITH AN OGRE

We couldn't go anywhere. Reports were now saying that roads were closed due to flooding. I was, quite frankly, sick and tired of rain. I decided I might as well cook dinner. The weather just called out for a big pot of chili and a pan of hot, buttermilk cornbread. I plugged in the slow cooker and set the oven to 375. I greased a pie pan with shortening and put it in the oven to heat.

Brett offered to help me in the kitchen. Pam was in the guest room Skyping with her grandchildren. Dan was watching golf and snuggling with Roxie. The storm had scared her inside. Brett stopped to look at the childhood pictures of my three that hung on the wall by the kitchen table.

I saw him looking at the pictures. "Remember when Leslie was so terrified of you?" I finished browning hamburger meat in a skillet and drained it good, before dumping it into the slow cooker.

"Yeah. It kind of hurt my feelings." Brett had a Vidalia onion on the cutting board and was expertly whacking at it.

"She thought you were an ogre." I laughed. "It was a combination of your size and your shiny bald head." I handed him a green bell pepper, fresh from Mom's garden.

"She eventually got over it. Your kids love me now." Brett diced the pepper and added it to the onions.

I opened two large cans of chopped, stewed tomatoes and one can of beans and poured the contents into my slow cooker. "Well, I remember that one Christmas."

Brett rolled his eyes. "You are getting as bad as Mom at bringing up corn stories." He added the vegetables from the cutting board to my tomato and hamburger mixture and rinsed off the cutting board.

I ignored that insult and handed him the garlic and cayenne, keeping a careful eye that he didn't add too much of either. "Remember how Leslie wouldn't come downstairs and open her presents with you in the living room? Even the sight of a new bicycle wouldn't lure her to join us." I took the cayenne away from him.

"I had to hide in the kitchen for an hour. Thank goodness, you had coffee cake." Brett stirred the chili, while I took a mixing bowl from the bottom cabinet.

"Dan was kind of miffed that you ate it all." I measured 4 cups of White Lily Cornmeal and put it in my bowl. I cracked two eggs and stirred them in, along with an ample amount of buttermilk.

Brett handed me the oil. "What was I supposed to do? You all were having fun opening presents, and I was just sitting in the cold kitchen, waiting."

I measured the oil carefully and added it to the cornmeal mixture. "Remember the Ogre in fairytales? I guess you had to know the password."

"I guess," he said. I let Brett have the honors of pulling the hot pie plate from the oven and pouring in my mix. We both enjoyed the nice sizzle as the cold cornmeal hit the hot oil.

I softened butter in the microwave and set it out with sour cream and a bowl of shredded cheese. "Didn't the three Billy Goats Gruff demand a password from the Ogre?"

Brett popped it back in the oven and asked me how long to set the timer. "No. That was not an Ogre. It was a Troll."

"Same thing." Kitchen duties done for a while, we went to join the rest of the family. I hoped the power would hold out. I knew I'd have hungry bellies if the chili and cornbread didn't cook properly.

CHAPTER 62
DAY 16

Cara flipped her sketchbook back to the squirrel eating a nut. She had drawn it the day of the picnic with her daddy. Under the nut she wrote, *I wish I had this nut. I'm hungry.* She was down to her last can of food. It was green beans, French style. Green beans were the worst food in the world to the little girl. They made her gag. And so, her daddy had never made her eat them. If he wanted some, he would make sure there was something else on the table for Cara. She loved peas.

"Why can't you be peas?" she said to the can. She wouldn't even have to scrape them on the rocks. Unlike all of the other cans, the green beans had an easy-to-open pull top lid. She knew she would eventually have to eat them. Before she did, she would search the car good for something else. She climbed into the front seat, and for the tenth time, tried to open the locked glove box. It wouldn't open.

Cara looked over at the ignition. The keys hung there still, even though the engine had died with the crash. She reached over and wiggled the keys until she had them free.

"Yay!" The key opened the glove box.

Cara rooted around inside the compartment and pulled everything out. There was a flashlight, a map of Georgia, and an owner's manual. No food. She flipped through the manual and was about to put it back when the cover drew her attention. There was a gold seal on the front. She carried the book and the flashlight to the back seat. Cara stored the flashlight in the backseat pocket. It would be nice to have at night. Using the knife, she cut away the seal from the front of the manual. Then she cut it into seven smaller pea-sized pieces and, licking them with her tongue, adhered them to the picture of the girl. She was very pleased.

For dinner, Cara used a rolled piece of paper from the owner's manual and scraped the sides of all of her empty cans. She sucked on the paper. It wasn't enough to still her hunger pangs, but it was better than green beans.

In the front seat, Teg moaned in his sleep.

When Teg was eighteen, he was dismissed by the courts. He'd received his high school diploma while he was at the residential treatment house. And now, he was free to do as he pleased.

He got a job in Atlanta, working at a factory on an assembly line. The factory made GM car parts, but sold them to all kinds of car makers, even overseas. Teg's job was to drill holes in brake rotors to prevent them from overheating or building up gasses. He mastered the heavy drilling machinery in no time. While the work was boring, he liked that it was manual and helped keep his muscles in shape. And he liked that he didn't have to talk to anybody. His foreman, Eddie Manning, wrote a good review on him during his probation period. He said Teg was a reliable worker, quick to learn, and had a good work ethic. He didn't write this in the evaluation, but privately, he appreciated that Teg was a quiet young man and stuck to his own business.

Teg had moved into a cheap furnished apartment near the factory. It had a cot and a small dresser with unreliable drawers that often had to be cobbled back together. The bathroom with its tiny shower wasn't big enough to spit in. The kitchen had undersized appliances including a dirty looking mini fridge. Teg didn't mind the place at first, even though there was a lot of traffic outside his door. For the next three years, drug dealers and hookers were his neighbors. He could hear them carrying on all night. He did his best to ignore them, went to work, and stayed out of trouble.

When Teg was finally twenty-one and old enough to drink, Eddie invited him for a beer. Teg had shrugged, "Why not?" It was at the bar that Teg first met Eunice. He didn't pay any mind to her at all. She was Eddie's sister and she was a dog. She plopped down at their table and drank with them and pretty much carried the conversation by herself.

"You work with Eddie, huh?"

Teg nodded his headed and signaled the waitress for another beer.

"Whatcha do there? You work the assembly?"

Eddie said, "What's with the questions, Eunice? I done told you he works with me."

"Just making conversation. That's all."

The table was quiet for a while as they listened to the music. A local band was playing, and they were pretty good. Teg watched the pretty lead singer with interest. She had auburn hair and a short skirt. He turned his chair so he could have a good view, and so he wouldn't have to look at Eunice.

Behind him, Eunice talked to Eddie.

"Amber wants you to come to her dance recital Friday night. You promised her."

"Yeah, yeah. I'll see what I can do."

"Look at her recital pictures. They came in the mail today. Ain't she pretty. She'll be eleven next month. I want you to come to her birthday party, too."

The waitress came over with Teg's beer and set a bowl of peanuts on the table. Teg turned around to grab a handful of nuts and saw the pictures that lay near Eddie. The girl was pretty. Brown hair to her shoulders and just budding breasts. She wore a variety of tight, clingy dance costumes . . . a different costume in each picture. The little girl had makeup on, too. Lots of it. He turned his chair back to the table and looked at Eunice a little closer. She smiled at him, exposing a layered triple chin and rotten teeth. Teg smiled back.

Eddie was delighted when Teg moved into the house with Eunice. He didn't care that there was no offer of marriage. Having Teg there to look after his sister and niece, took a huge burden off of him. Let Teg fix the leaky sink and the falling side boards. His sister needed a man, and she'd gone and got herself a good one. Eddie was pleased.

CHAPTER 63
FLOODS

The power flickered on and off a few times. But, we were able to enjoy a wonderful warm dinner of chili and cornbread. The cornbread had risen beautifully, and I cut it into nice perfect wedges. I never know. Sometimes my cornbread is too crumbly. Thankfully, that night it held together just right. It was delicious, especially with hot, melted, oozing salted butter. The chili was a little too spicy . . . Thank you, Brett . . . but the sour cream and cheese helped dilute the cayenne. Overall, it was a delightful dinner and everyone had second helpings.

Pam had peach cobbler she had made at home from the fruit of her peach tree. She had snuck it in, and hidden it in my deep freezer when she first arrived. She popped it into my still hot oven to heat. What a nice surprise! We would have that later with ice cream if any of us still had room and if the power continued to hold.

Massive flash flooding was reported everywhere in the Southeast. Trees were falling, roads were washing out, and power lines were down. We all wondered about Cara. Did she have food? Was she warm? Was she safe? We didn't know. We were losing hope.

CHAPTER 64
DAY 17

Its raining hard today. My pee is in a bag and needs to be dumped out. But the rain will come in if I open the door. Im very hungry to. I need to open the green beans but I just cant. God must no Ill throw up if I eat them. But Im so hungry. I ll eat them tomorrow may be.

Mr. Duke is talking in his sleep again. He is saying really gross things that I wont write about. Its about a girl named Amber. He says hes just having a date. But it is really awful so Im staying in back today and drawing. My picture of the girl is finished and I don't have any more pages, but I can make little pictures on the edges of the other pages. I keep telling Mr. Duke to hush up. I cant stand the stuff hes saying. Its nasty and I dont belive it either.

There is a lot of thunder and litening. Its very scarey here. My head hurts bad.

Cara crawled under the upholstery. Her hand hurt badly, now. A thin line of red was moving up her wrist. Her head pounded. She shivered with cold chills. She didn't know it, but she was running a fever, the hand infected. She slept restlessly throughout the storm. Teg did the same in the front seat, occasionally shouting out in his sleep. Cara could hear him, but she felt too bad to care.

CHAPTER 65
SEARCHING

The rain finally drizzled out in the early morning. I could tell by the clocks that we had, indeed, lost power sometime during the night. I would let Dan reset them all. Roxie was standing by the French doors ready to go out. She had been cooped up all night in the house, and I happily obliged her. The sun was up, and I was thrilled as I could be to see a blue sky.

Dan had already left for work and had coffee made in the percolator. For once, I was raring to go. I banged on their doors, to rouse up my brother and sister.

We had arranged the night before to meet at Leman's house to organize. Lizzie was already there when we arrived. Pam brought Leman a plastic container of her peach cobbler. He thanked her like a gentleman and put it in his refrigerator. I doubted he would eat it, though. We could all tell he was losing weight. I bet he hadn't had a proper meal since Cara disappeared.

I also knew the flood waters would be bad, and there would be very few searchers out. Even so, we were willing to try. Without asking first, Pam and I rummaged through the cabinets and refrigerator to try to find something we could make Leman for breakfast. We were determined to get him to eat something before we left.

Leman didn't stop us and actually nibbled some buttered toast that Pam made while I scrambled some eggs. Pam cut a small piece of the cobbler and heated it in the microwave. The *Cara* license plate sat on the counter.

While we cooked, Leman had a map of Georgia spread open on the kitchen table. He had drawn lines and written notes all over the map with a red marker and a yellow highlighter. Nearby, was a laptop that he used to scan Google Earth during times he wasn't out in his truck. Leman, Lizzie, and Brett were studying the map when the house phone rang.

CHAPTER 66
DAY 18

Teg dreamed of Eunice. He dreamed of her flabby body that folded around him, crushing him. He dreamed of the bad breath that stewed in her rotten teeth. And he dreamed of Amber. As he reached for her, the little girl faded away, and Teg dreamed of his mother. He dreamed of her gentle hand, the country songs in a low alto voice, standing by her side at the sink. His mother protecting him from the bad. He could see the golden curls that sparkled as she kissed his cheek.

Cara dreamed, too. She dreamed of her room at home, her pink bedspread and her framed posters of horses and puppies. She had a ribbon on the corner of her bulletin board that she had won in the class spelling bee. She dreamed of her daddy. He was helping her sharpen her colored pencils. Her daddy was wearing a funny hat. He had won it at the carnival over at the VFW fairgrounds playing skee ball. He had tried his best to win Cara a bear. Instead, he ended up with the hat. It had a propeller on top, and Cara thought it was hilarious and made him wear it. And she dreamed of the lady. The lady wanted more gold sparkles on everything. Cara tried to tell her they were all gone, but she said to please keep trying.

Cara awoke, coughing. Her head still hurt and she needed to pee. She emptied the bag from the day before and did her business behind the driver's seat. It burned when she peed. She couldn't open the door to empty the bag. The creek had risen above the wheels and pressed against the door, and regardless, she just didn't have the strength.

She heard Teg moaning. Despite how she felt, she knew he needed water, badly. So did she.

Cara forced her aching body to climb over the console with the rain boot. She held it to Teg's lips and he drank a small amount. He looked at her yellowing eyes. Then he saw the red streak up her arm. His feet were wet. He could tell water was seeping into the car. Soon, they would be flooded.

He said, "Lick it."

"Lick what?" Cara didn't understand.

It was a struggle for him to talk. His voice was near a whisper, and Cara could hear a rattling in his chest as he spoke each word. "The phone. Get the phone and lick the battery."

This made no sense at all. But, Cara reached over and retrieved the phone from the back storage pocket. She looked all around it for where the battery might be. She finally found a latch that opened and showed it to the man.

"Is this it?"

He nodded. "Take it out and lick it."

Cara did. She felt a tingling on her tongue.

"Now, put it back in. Try calling your daddy."

Cara was surprised, but she flipped the phone open and pushed the power button. The phone lit up.

"Call quick. Not much time."

Cara dialed the house number. It rang.

CHAPTER 67
CALLING HOME

Leman left the map to answer the phone. He was still talking as he picked up the receiver. "I think if we head further upstream . . ."

"Daddy!"

"Oh my . . . Cara!"

We all stopped and gathered around.

"Where are you, honey?"

"I don't know, Daddy. I'm in the car with Mr. Duke. He's hurt bad. We are stuck down deep in the rocks. There is a river under us, and it is getting higher like you said it would. I think water is coming inside the car. The floor is wet."

Leman heard a man coughing and then a male voice said something . . . unintelligible . . . He could hear the man but had difficulty understanding him. Something he couldn't make out . . . then "Shoal" . . . then something else . . .

"Did he hurt you? What did he say, Cara? Ask him where you are." Leman tried not to sound panicked, but he couldn't help it.

"Daddy, I . . ."

The phone went dead, again.

Leman was on fire. "I could just hear shoals, and then I lost her again. A man . . . some man was saying shoals, I think. Some man has my daughter!"

Brett ran over to the laptop and brought up Google. He typed in *Georgia shoals*. His entry brought up sites for *High Fall Shoals* in both Hiawassee and Dallas, *Hurricane Shoals Park* in Maysville, *Factory Shoals* in Lithia Springs, and *Scull Shoals* in Greensboro. Lizzie grabbed the marker and began circling the areas on the map.

I called the Carrollton Police and asked for officer Chad. It took forever for someone to get him to the phone. Finally, he answered, and I told him about the call. He wrote down everything and said he would contact various police agencies to get them searching those areas. He was excited and energized by the news. So were we.

Leman wanted to drive to Dallas first and look there. Lizzie and Pam agreed to ride with him.

I asked, "Where should we go?" It made sense for Brett and me to go somewhere else. "I was thinking Lithia Springs." We three Gardin kids had gone to high school there, and we were familiar with the area.

Brett was looking at the map. His forehead wrinkled in the same way that my father's used to look when he studied a problem. He was pointing to a spot in Alabama.

Brett said, "This may not make much sense to the rest of you. See this area, over the state line? I seem to remember a place near there named something shoal or shoal something." He went to the computer again and typed in *Shoals Alabama*. This time there were numerous sites for *Muscle Shoals, Alabama*.

Brett shook his head, no. "There's some place closer. I just can't think what it is. I remember a lot of rocky crevices."

Pam suggested, "Remove the s and just type in *shoal*."

Brett did as she said, and came to a site for *Shoal Creek*. "That's it. Let's go there and look."

We programmed the directions into the GPS of my phone. As we got into my car, Leman handed Brett a big loop of rope and some blankets. "Take this," he said. "Just in case." Leman had another rope that he carried to his car. Pam and Lizzie each carried a blanket. Pam rode up front with Leman, Lizzie in the back seat.

Brett dropped the rope and blankets behind him in the back, and we pulled out of Leman's driveway turning left toward the back roads that would take us to Bowdon and then Alabama. I let Brett drive as he seemed to know better where we were going. I wouldn't have agreed to that if I'd known then that we would be on mountain roads. Leman turned right. He would be taking I-20 or Highway 92, I assumed, to get to Dallas. There was excitement all around. At least we had some new places to look and, for now, we knew Cara was alive!

CHAPTER 68
BYE BYE MEAN MAN

Cara closed the phone with a sigh. She hoped the call helped, but she didn't think it would. She couldn't tell her daddy where she was because she didn't know. And her head hurt terribly bad. White stuff was coming out of the cuts on her fingers. She stared at her swollen, sore hand for a few seconds, feeling dizzy. She looked over at Mr. Duke. His head had fallen to the side, and he was staring at her with glazed, lifeless eyes. His mouth hung open, and a fly crawled from his lip to his drying tongue.

"Bye Bye, mean man. I guess you've gone to where the bad people go."

She stayed there for a while, her head spinning. Blow flies began crawling through the air vents. They landed on Teg's face and chest. More came. Soon there were dozens swarming over the dead body. It was too much for the little girl.

Cara climbed into the backseat and under her upholstery spread. She felt like crying, but the tears just wouldn't come. She had heard her daddy's voice. That was a good thing. Cara's lips were cracked from fever, but she had no energy left to get water. She shivered in and out of sleep.

CHAPTER 69
SHOAL CREEK OGRE

I called Dan at work to let him know what was going on.

"Wow. No kidding?"

"Seriously. She called her dad. We could hear some of it. The police are looking at all the places with Shoals in their name. There's a lot more than you would think."

"I'm assuming you will wait for the police if you find anything. Keep me posted and be careful. I love you."

"Love you, too. Go earn some money so you can buy me a duvet."

He laughed as he hung up.

It took us the better part of an hour to reach the Shoal Creek area. I got a little queasy as Brett rounded the rocky curves and the car climbed higher.

My phone rang again. It was Lizzie calling.

"Hey, you guys find anything?" I asked.

"No. We are sitting at a gas station on 92. Your crazy sister is insisting that we turn around and come to where you are."

"Let me talk to her."

Pam took the phone.

"Penny, she's there. Where you are. And she has a painting . . . or a drawing of a painting. It's just like yours. It even has the gold sparkles."

"Are you sure?"

"Yes. I'm sure."

"Put me on speaker phone."

She did.

I said, "Leman, I know you don't know us very well. But, you asked for my help in Walmart that day, because you read those articles about us. You need to trust me now, and you need to trust Pam. She gets these weird intuition things, that I don't understand, and she's almost always right. Well, not about Donald Trump being President in a few years. But most of the time, she's right."

I heard a quiet and puzzled, "Okay."

I gave them directions that I echoed from Brett's instruction beside me. I could tell my brother was relieved that they were coming. Brett had apparently had an intuition of his own, or we wouldn't be climbing this mountain.

I cracked my window hoping the cool air would stifle my car sickness. The nausea was coming in waves. The roads were narrow, and there wasn't much of a shoulder on either side.

I know my face was turning green. "Brett! Lord Jesus, riding on the back of a donkey through the streets of Jerusalem . . . Please slow down on these curves."

"Sorry. You getting sick? We could pull over somewhere and walk."

"Yes . . . No . . . Stop, if you see something. There's no shoulder. Where in the world would we pull over?" I rolled the window all the way down and hung my head out like a panting dog.

"I was wondering the same thing. Oh, wait! There's one of those scenic tourist spots."

A small parking area had been cut on the side. Two telescopes on mounts had been installed there to view the gorgeous landscape.

He pulled the car over. I was grateful to get out. I leaned over with my head between my knees until the nausea passed. Brett opened the back door and took out the rope. He left the blankets in the car and shut the door. The rope, he slung over his shoulder. We took advantage of the equipment at hand and scanned the terrain with the telescopes. We saw nothing of the SUV.

"Let's walk," Brett said.

"Glad to." I felt better out of the car and in the open air.

We walked up the road on the left side so that we could see down the embankment. A few cars drove by, and we froze. Not a lot of room there for us to get out of the way. A misstep on the gravely shoulder, and we had a long way to fall. The rising creek roared forty feet below us.

We walked about fifteen minutes, barely missing getting creamed by a semi. The driver blared his horn at us. The wind created by the big truck nearly pushed me over the side, and would have, if Brett hadn't grabbed me. Thankfully, I could see a rocky outcropping ahead. It looked like a tunnel but was open at the top and its lower rocks provided a natural bench.

We sat on the edge of the rocks to catch our breath.

"I don't think we can keep doing this. It's dangerous."

"It is. I know. Let's just walk a little further."

"Okay."

We stayed close to the rocks. They shielded us from the edge at least. We came to a sharp curve and Brett said, "Look here."

We could see scrapes of black paint on the rock. Someone had, maybe, sideswiped their car here. Brett followed me out of the outcropping, and we were back on a narrow shoulder again.

The sun sparkled and radiated off of the rocks, nearly blinding us. A few feet further, and I spotted something down below. Light reflected back at us, bouncing off of a mirror. We stopped, shielding our eyes. We could see the top of a large black vehicle wedged between the rocks. The creek had risen underneath the car. From our view, we couldn't tell if the water was high enough to flood the vehicle, but it had to be close. "Dear Lord and your sweet Heavenly Mother wrapped in a silken shawl," I said. "I think we found them."

I called Lizzie's phone to let them know. I had to wait for them all to hush so I could give directions. I couldn't blame them for being excited. I couldn't imagine how Leman was feeling.

I could see a stretch ahead with another pull off area. "When you get here, go past where you see my car parked. Drive a couple of miles until you pass through something like a rock tunnel. You will see a place you can park just ahead of it. We will be across and a little down from there." Then I called 911 and told the local police where we were, and that we would need a rescue team. My last call was to Chad. He would coordinate with the Alabama State Police as he drove to the state line.

Brett was studying the terrain below. "I'm not waiting for the police." He began tying the rope around his waist. The other end, he tied to a tree at the edge of the ravine. The tree was young, its girth around six inches. I doubted it had been there long enough to establish much of a root system. I was certainly skeptical that it could hold my brother.

I said, "No, Brett. Please. Do not do this. Just wait. Help will be here soon."

Did he listen to me? Nope. He tested the rope, and satisfied that it would hold him, my crazy brother began rappelling down the rocks. Small stones immediately broke loose under his feet and fell onto the roof of the car below. I clung to the tree and watched him as he descended. Brett had looped the rope and was feeding it a little at a time as he climbed down. I held my breath. We didn't even know if the rope was long enough.

The little tree Brett had tied the rope to was strong enough. It didn't bend at all from his weight. But, the ground underneath, saturated from weeks of rain, began to fall away. Clumps of dirt and larger stones broke loose from the ravine's fragile edge. One huge clod of dirt hit the top of Brett's bald head and exploded. He just shook it off and kept going. Meanwhile, I could see more and more root exposed below. With each foot Brett descended, more dirt fell from underneath the tree.

Cara heard the thuds of stone and dirt hitting the car hood. She sat up and listened. She climbed up over the console. The blow flies were everywhere, but she did her best to ignore them and Mr. Duke. She tried, unsuccessfully, to see up through the front windshield. More rocks fell. One cracked the windshield right in front of her, and startled, she fell back behind the console.

Brett yelped a few times as rocks bounced off of his chest and stomach. The tree leaned forward over the ravine, dropping Brett about five or six feet. The entire root was now exposed and little was left to keep it anchored. I still had my arms around the trunk. I was leaning forward with it, trying my best to hold it in place. I heard Brett yelling at me to let go. So I did.

Brett and I both knew that the tree was going to fall. I screamed and screamed for him to hurry and he began rappelling faster. He was about six feet from the car when the earth gave up and the tree let go. Brett dropped onto the car hood with a loud thud, rocking the SUV. He grabbed hold of a windshield wiper and held on. Then my brother wisely took out his knife and cut the rope loose.

The tree wavered a few more times and then crashed into the creek below. It was gone from sight in seconds in the fast flowing water. My heart had nearly stopped by then. I was too far up to see, but I could imagine his dirt covered face and the fear in his eyes. And, I had no idea what danger Brett still faced inside of the car.

Brett knelt on the hood and peered into the window. He could see Teg in the driver's seat. Blow flies covered the dead man's face. Brett knew he wouldn't need the knife anymore and put it in his pocket.

Cara was terrified by the sounds and tremors of my brother and the tree hitting the car. Then, she saw the dirt covered big man with the bald head staring at her and screamed. She climbed over the back seat and scrambled to the hatch. She cowered in the back of the cargo, still screaming.

Brett yelled up at me. "I see her. Bad guy's dead. And she's screaming."

"What?" I couldn't hear him well over the rush of the creek.

"BAD GUY IS DEAD. SHE'S SCREAMING! WHAT SHOULD I DO?"

Poor Cara. I could imagine what she thought with Brett landing on the car hood like that. I yelled back, "She thinks you are an ogre."

"What?"

"SHE THINKS YOU ARE AN OGRE!"

"WHAT DO I DO?"

"I DON'T KNOW. SAY SOMETHING NICE."

Brett cupped his hands around his mouth and yelled at Cara. "Hey, little girl. Hey, Cara. I'm here to get you."

Cara screamed louder. Even I could hear her that time. I thought for a few seconds and then remembered something Leman had told us.

"SAY COUNTY FAIR. IT'S A PASSWORD."

Brett tried that. He yelled "COUNTY FAIR" over and over at the window.

Cara stopped screaming and peeked over the seat. Whoever this scary stranger was, her daddy had sent him. Slowly, shaking, she climbed from the hatch forward to the back seat.

Brett told her to stay where she was. He used his foot to stomp the glass on the window where it had cracked. He teetered a few times and came close to falling into the creek. Despite that, he soon had a good sized hole. He continued to kick the safety glass and used his hands to pull some of it away. The safety glass pulled away in big chunks. When he could, he climbed through to the front seat. He avoided looking at Teg and swatted at the flies that buzzed nearby.

Brett spoke softly to Cara. "Hi, Cara. I'm Brett. I'm a nurse, and I'm a friend of your father. He's on his way here to get you. Are you okay?"

Cara nodded and showed him her hand. Gently, he examined her. She was burning up with fever. It looked bad, and Brett knew she needed IV antibiotics. The blood poison was seeping up her arm.

"I'm going to get you out of here. Okay?"

Cara nodded again. She let Brett hug her and soon, her shaking stopped. He held her in his arms, talking to her, keeping her warm, as he waited for rescue.

Police cars and ambulances arrived. I talked to the rescue team and told them who we were. EMTs lowered a safety basket and blanket down to Brett. He wrapped Cara warmly and loaded her into the basket. I was standing close by when they brought her up.

Cara's eyes locked into mine. She said, "I know you! I know you! I need my backpack. Please get my backpack. It has my drawing of the little girl with the gold sparkles. It's just like yours, I dreamed it."

I didn't know what to think. The child was delirious. I yelled her request down to Brett, and he waved the backpack to show me that he had it. The rescue team would have fun getting him back up the rocks.

Cara was placed in the back of the ambulance. She said, "Please, let that lady come with me." I climbed in beside her.

An EMT inserted an IV into Cara's arm. She hardly noticed. "Do you know my daddy?"

"I do, honey. He's been looking for you, and he will be here soon."

"You're that lady. I dreamed about you."

"You did? I'm Penny." I was so confused.

"You told me to put gold sparkles."

"Oh, my! Cara are you sure it was me? Did you dream this?"

She nodded. "I don't think she has a name . . . the girl in my drawing. I think she's an angel up in Heaven."

I liked that. "Oh, Cara . . . I wasn't sure who I was painting, either. And I think she's an angel in mine, too. I would love to see your drawing."

She smiled weakly. "It's in my backpack. Please get it." She opened her thin little arms.

I leaned over and, despite the IV, Cara clasped her arms around my neck, squeezing tight. I knew the child was traumatized, terrified still, but I could feel her strength, despite the fever. She was an artist. She'd be all right.

Cara whispered, "And I didn't have to eat the green beans."

I heard another siren. The police had escorted Leman to the pull off. He jumped out of the car and ran to the ambulance. Pam and Lizzie stood on the ravine, a good distance away, and watched the rescue team struggle to fit our great big little brother into a harness. I climbed out of the ambulance, and let Leman take my place beside his daughter. They were both crying. Leman handed me his keys. He would ride to the hospital in the ambulance. They pulled away, lights flashing.

I walked over to Lizzie and Pam and waited for Brett to join us. My big ogre of a brother was still a challenge for the rescue squad trying to lift him. As we waited, I couldn't help but think that if my microwave hadn't died, I might not have met Leman, and maybe this child wouldn't have been found in time. What a silly, trivial thing . . . a dead microwave. Funny how life happens.

When Brett finally made it to the top of the road, backpack in hand, we hugged. All four of us. Lizzie wanted to see the drawing. I was hesitant to pry, but Cara had said I could. We opened the pack and pulled out the sketch pad. We flipped through, and like Leman, we were amazed at her drawings and writings. On the last page, we found the picture of the girl. Though not at all an exact copy, the similarity to mine was stunning.

Pam looked at it and said, "I think you have an artist twin."

"She's more like you, Pam. She has your very weird intuition thing, I think. I just painted a painting."

We took the backpack with the sketchpad to the hospital. Pam drove Leman's car, and we left it there in the parking lot for him. We visited with Leman for a few minutes and then drove home, exhausted.

Dan was at the house when we arrived with celebratory steaks on the grill and baked potatoes in the microwave oven. He was tossing a salad with oil and red wine vinegar. Roxie was asleep on my dad's set of World Book Encyclopedias on the top of the bookshelf. Her body stretched from F to M. Good spot for her. She was too far up to scratch me. It was great to be home, again.

EPILOGUE

My siblings and I received a lot of publicity for helping find Cara, which I hated, and Pam and Brett loved. At least this time we weren't in any danger. Well, sure, Pam nearly got snake bit by a venomous serpent, Brett plunged off a cliff and nearly fell to his death, and I got mauled by my mentally ill cat. But, these are normal occurrences in our family. And, really, who hasn't experienced those things?

ॐ ⑩ ॐ

Leman Garrett dropped Cara off at the Blue Heron. He brought her to us every Thursday after school, and let us keep her for a couple of hours. Cara was embraced by all of her adopted aunts and grandmothers. Eventually, Cara would move to Tuesdays with the other children. But for now, she was ours. There is no place on Earth that can soothe and heal one's soul like that little studio. Melanie's daughter, April, likes to remind us that well people are welcome, too. Even so, there are many of us who come for therapeutic laughter and friendship, and the healing that comes from losing one's self in artistic creation.

Melissa took a cutting wire, sliced a piece of Georgia red clay, and sat it on the huge slab roller. Cara, unaided, dug through the form shelf and selected a small platter and a bit of lace. Melissa helped her position the lace on the clay and covered it with canvas. Cara was strong enough now to turn the rod that moved the roller across her slab of clay, flattening and compressing it into an acceptable thickness. We watched Cara as the canvas and lace were removed. She was delighted with the result. Kyra stepped in to help position the clay, lace side down, on the platter form. Melanie provided tools and instruction on sculpting the edges and compressing any air pockets.

All the while, Cara told us about her day at school. She had made an A on a short story about a lost baby deer in the woods.

Her little face lit up describing her wonderful and caring teacher who had encouraged her to share the story with her classmates. And that wasn't all! Her daddy had surprised her with a fresh peach in her lunch box, and she just loved peaches. Later in the afternoon, a few children on the playground had said some mean things, repeating what they had probably heard from their parents. Cara's face darkened as she told us. We were good listeners, and if she needed to cry a little, we cried with her.

Cara sat between me and Lizzie in a rickety cane back chair, a smile on her face, and Molly curled at her feet. I adjusted the old Atlanta phone book in her seat so that she could reach the table. Smells of Melanie's sweet potato soup drifted in from the kitchen. Kyra had brought a pan of cornbread, and Sherry had made a blueberry pie. Honey helped set the table on the front porch. It was a beautiful night to eat outdoors. Dinner would be ready soon, but we had work to do first.

Cara lightly carved a shape of the deer from her short story into the clay. We admired her detail and skill as we worked on our own pieces. Sometimes, we were all quiet, absorbed in our art, and sometimes, we weren't. Conversation and laughter came in spits and spatters. When Cara was finished with her carving, Sweet Emily poured black underglaze into one of Molly's recycled dog food dishes. Dulcie supplied fresh water, a sponge, and a fan brush. Together, through giggles and chatter, we began teaching Cara a new lesson in the fine art of Sgraffito pottery.

I returned home from the Blue Heron late, nearly midnight. Dan was in bed asleep. Roxie was draped, again, across the rungs of a kitchen chair. Her head rested in peaceful slumber on the cold floor. I sat my purse and basket of glazed pottery on the counter and froze. There was a Post-it note on my beloved percolator. It said, "Coffee maker is dead."

Lord.

THANK YOU

To my very tolerant family, who provide so much writing material that I could fill volumes: Dan, Meagan, Leslie, Chris, Mom (Betty), Nancy, Pam, and Brett.

To friends Kathy Waldrop, Louise Garrett, and Melonie Hopkins who patiently let me read aloud to them, an important part of my process.

To John Bell and Staff of Vabella Publishing.

To Lisa Matheson, Chief Creative Director, Black Squirrel Art Company

To Larry Johnson for his guidance and edits.

To my editor, good friend, and mentor, Dr. Eleanor Hoomes

And an extra very special thank you to Cover Artist, C. Louise Garrett (Gentry)

ABOUT THE AUTHOR

Penny Lewis is a Berry College graduate. She is a former Industrial Arts Teacher and later, the director of the Carrollton Cultural Arts Center. She and husband Dan have written and produced 38 musicals for children. They are parents to grown and gone children Meagan, Leslie, and Chris and currently live in Carrollton, Georgia with their mentally ill cat Roxie and rescue goldfish Judy. Penny is enjoying retirement, writing novels, and making pottery at the Blue Heron. This is her second novel.

CONTACT PENNY

For interviews and other publicity matters or arrange speaking or reading engagements contact:

Lisa Matheson, Publicist
Crisis Whisperer, LLC
lisa@crisiswhisperer.com

To write to the author directly, inquire about attendance at book clubs or find out how to obtain an autographed copy of her books contact: info@PennyLewis.press

Let's Connect!
https://www.facebook.com/PenLewis

https://twitter.com/pennylewispress

https://instagram.com/pennylewispress

Please enjoy this little snippet from Penny's next novel.

DEAR CRABIGAIL
PROLOGUE
24 Years Earlier

She kissed his forehead. April loved the way her man looked when he slept, so at peace. Like her, Adam was a neurosurgeon and they both spent long hours in the operating room. April needed sleep, too. But the babies in her womb had begun moving and she savored the feeling. She rubbed her stomach gently. The double butterfly flutterings within made her smile.

They had met at a Starbucks across from the hospital on her first day of residency, laughing at the identical orders, a caramel macchiato with whipped cream and a sprinkle of cinnamon. Adam had said, "I guess we're twins. Care to share a table?" And she had, drawn by his deep blue eyes and wispy blond hair. Likewise, he was captivated by her charming smile, her short dark hair...so dark it was nearly black and piercing brown eyes with flecks of gold. April was tall, nearly as tall as he with a svelte figure and perky breasts. Not too big, not too small. Adam was in love instantly. More so when he learned over that cup of coffee that they shared the same profession. He liked his women smart.

Physical attraction was important, but they both enjoyed long discussions about politics, the environment, and art. They had graduated at the top of their classes and were respected in their matching professions.

April couldn't resist kissing the same spot again on Adam's forehead. He murmured something. She couldn't tell what it was. He didn't seem disturbed. She looked at the clock. It was nearly 90 minutes since he'd fallen asleep and soon he would enter the REM stage. His eyelid flutters would match those in her womb.

She reached under her pillow and pulled out a large five-inch nail tied to a string. Her grandmother had taught her this trick many years ago. To determine the sex of a child you twirl the suspended nail and wait for it to settle into a rhythm. And when it did, you looked at which way it swung. If it moved back and forth, the baby, or in this case, babies, would be boys. If the pendulum moved around in circles then the babies would be girls. April didn't know what it would do if she were pregnant with one of each. Adam would scoff at this old wives' tale if he knew, but April didn't care. She held the nail above his forehead, right over the spot where she had kissed him twice.

The nail twirled for a couple of minutes until it began to find its rhythm. When the nail showed her what it wanted to reveal, April smiled. She rested the tip of the nail on Adam's brow, on the sweet kissed spot. And then retrieving a hammer from under the pillow, she drove the nail deep into his head.

CHAPTER 1

Dear Crabigail,
I have good reason to believe that my neighbor across the street has stolen my rocking chair right off of my front porch. I spend many hours there each day, watching and feeding birds. Should I confront her or call the police?
Sincerely, Off Her Rocker in Cincinnati

Dear Off Your Rocker,
Sounds to me like your good neighbor has gone and done you a favor. If you are spending all day sitting on that porch like you say, then you ain't getting any exercise and you are packing on the pounds. If that's the case, then by now, your thighs are probably squeezing out the sides of that rocker and embarrassing the whole neighborhood. So get yourself up and do some jumping jacks and

sit squats. If you can't do that, then I suggest buying a porch swing so them thighs of yours has more room to spread out.

Yours, Crabigail

Dear Crabigail
If you're interested in Crabigail's unique brand of sassy, unvarnished advice, please write her at:

advice@dearcrabigail.com

Don't hold your breath waiting for a reply though. She′ll get to you when she gets to you. And if she does, you might just end up in the book!

DEAR CRABIGAIL

By Penny Gardin Lewis
Third Book in the Series due this Fall

Twins Penny and Pam are hot on the trail of an evil serial killer, this time for their own preservation. While Penny has tried her best to lay low, Pam has become somewhat infamous as the writer of a "Dear Crabigail" Advice Column. Her notoriety may have made her a target of the murderer who specifically seeks out twins as victims.

IF YOU LIKED THIS BOOK AND HAVEN'T READ THE FIRST ONE, LOOK FOR

www.ingramcontent.com/pod-product-compliance
Lightning Source LLC
Chambersburg PA
CBHW071237260626
47159CB00005BA/1783